Summer's Swarm

Books by Andean White

Winter's Thief

Spring's Saboteurs

Summer's Swarm

Autumn's Rescue
(Coming Soon)

Summer's Swarm

Book 3

ANDEAN WHITE

Idea Creations Press
www.ideacreationspress.com

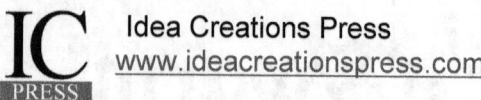

Idea Creations Press
www.ideacreationspress.com

This is a work of fiction. Any resemblance of characters to actual persons, living or dead, is purely coincidental.

Library of Congress Control Number: 2016945714

ISBN-13: 9780996665766
ISBN-10: 0996665765

Printed in the U.S.A.

Dedication

Fearless
A mom
Explorer
Example
Smart
My Sister
Kid-do
Robin

Thank you!

Acknowledgements

This is my third book and I'm still surprised at the number of people it takes to publish a book—readers, editors, technicians, graphics, marketing and web administration. And, I am truly grateful for everyone's input and skills.

To Dale George who joined the Andean White Book's team recently, I am very thankful for your detailed review.

Kathryn Elizabeth Jones, your patience is much appreciated. Thank you for the many challenges and never compromising your high standards.

Thanks to Douglas Jones for preparing the eBook and soft cover versions of the book. It has to be magic because I send Doug ten files and he returns a book.

In the past I have sent graphic artist Nathan Paret stick figure drawings that he turned into a book cover. For this book he received a description over lunch. It appears that the less I give him the better his work. "Nate, I am thinking about the fourth book's cover..."

Corporal Punishment

Head Master George Ulster's large hand grabbed Luxton's long black hair and lifted him to his tiptoes. He hauled him across the cake and icing, then out the sheet skirted dining room into the converted confessional area where a lone chair was fixed to the floor. Mid-afternoon meant Luxton could focus on the stained glass dove cast on the west sheet and dream of flying away on its back. A hundred plus heads would watch through the *walls'* seams.

Without a word, Luxton gripped the edge of the seat; Ulster whipped.

Luxton heard the head master's angry grumbling, uncertain what Ulster said to himself with each sting of the whip. Cutting more skin, Luxton thought about the happy moments preceding this event.

He seemed unable to create such turmoil. Luxton Pakrimi looked sixteen—a foot taller and a muscular thirty-five pounds more than other thirteen year olds. His shy wide eyes, smooth nose and large mouth created a perception of innocence and his big smile complemented the look.

He had become the target of the desperate head master. The open whipping along with the confinement set a tone that kept the other boys in line, particularly the misfits—the group of thirteen teenage boys responsible for pranks and vandalism.

It had become worse when Ulster, at the Archbishop's *request*, re-instated the monthly 'birthday' celebration. The first miniature festival for the twenty-three orphans with June dates was scheduled for the sixteenth.

Trying to coordinate enough cake pieces for two hundred thirty-nine orphans in an eighty-four seat dining area proved to be on the edge of insanity.

A line for boys and another for girls formed in the middle between the narrow tables.

Luxton, who was turning fourteen on June twenty-six, gave up his priority position and stepped to the end of the line as an act of defiance. At the end of the girl's line he stood beside Molly—nine, black hair, sweet hazel eyes, an attractive smile and a crippled leg.

"What is your date?" Luxton asked.

"November twelve," Molly replied. "How long has it been for you?"

She stumbled over a loose floor stone. Luxton caught her and helped her stand.

"I have been here for nine years. It was okay until a few years ago when Lady Lee died. She would convince the merchants to donate clothing and food."

They advanced another five feet. Molly tripped again.

"I would be honored to carry you to the cake," Luxton said.

"Oh, that would be nice."

Luxton cradled Molly in his arms. "We are about twenty people from the cake. I hope they do not run out. Cake is a nice change."

Molly patted Luxton's shoulder, "Thank you. I would probably trip and drop my cake before finding a seat."

"You are welcome."

They were the last two and Sister Margret Ann gave her last piece of cake to Molly. Luxton turned Molly toward the head master for his cake; Ulster wrinkled his nose and swallowed hard while swinging cake between Molly and the baking pan. Ulster acquiesced, but averted his gaze.

Molly's reach was a mere inch too short. She caught enough to juggle the corner morsel into Luxton's chest. His belly laugh triggered the release of the collected tensions of two hundred thirty-nine orphans.

A food fight ensued.

The flying white cake reminded Luxton of snow being whisked about by a cold wind.

Luxton's laughter and the frosting splattered on Ulster's clothes, raised his ire. The emotional monsoon that preceded Ulster's disciplinary actions meant one thing to Luxton—another public whipping. He set Molly gently on the end of the bench seat before he turned to run. Ulster caught his collar but it ripped away from the shirt—further maddening the head master.

When Luxton slipped on the frosting littered floor, he knew he had lost, again!

Nazar Cathedral, established twenty years ago by the Celestial Glory Church in the remote wilderness of Dashald, had been built for the purpose of *taking God to the barbarians*. It quickly became the central unifying structure for the rickety village that sprung up along the turbulent river.

Ten years ago, the church had converted rapidly to an orphanage when the river dwindled to a stream during the eighteen-month drought. Many families left children at the cathedral steps and departed overnight. The head master gave each orphan a name and recorded birthdays as the date they entered the orphanage.

Ropes and sheets crisscrossing the Nave established walls for boys' dormitory, girls' sleeping quarters, nursery, a small dining room, a cramped classroom, narrow hallways and makeshift washrooms.

The trio of past annual visits ended with the territorial archbishop scolding Ulster for hours over the "deplorable conditions".

Contributing to sleepless nights taking its toll on Ulster's health was pressure from the territorial archbishop—along with the caring of too many children, the dwindling food and clothing donations and the vandalizing and pranks by the older misfit boys. These were a few of the troubles that revealed his tortured soul.

Ulster's skin had a grayish white coloration. His eyes were a permanent red and his former well-fitting clothes hung off his shoulders—he looked like a tall orphan.

The annual clothing donation gathered by the archbishop arrived in the morning. Two boys, one a misfit and three girls sorted the clothes by size, female, male and needing repair. The shipment contained worn-out clothes, boldly colored apparel, laced collars and dirt stains. The variety of dress at meals and classrooms looked like a mucky spring assortment of wild flowers.

The misfit hid five of the nicest drab shirts in the sorting area for retrieval later, then carried the shirts to Luxton's cot. He looked in every direction before packing them under the cot. Luxton watched the whole episode.

Not wanting another whipping, Luxton waited for the misfit to depart. He checked the area and was satisfied he was alone.

He was removing the fifth shirt when the head master walked up from behind. Ulster did not wait or say anything.

He grabbed Luxton's legs and dragged him to the modified confessional. "You are too much trouble for this orphanage. You need to change your attitude, mister. Maybe a week of confinement will be a good start," Ulster said loudly as though he was making announcements before church.

"But, I did not steal them, I was going to return them to the shipment." Luxton replied. He glanced about grabbing the chair and table legs.

"Sure you were."

Arriving at the confessional Luxton stood and fought, his arms and feet flailing, attempting to escape Ulster's grip. He had lost the effort, but discovered he would soon have enough strength to defeat Ulster. When the door was locked, Luxton remembered there was no place to sit.

Luxton had a week to plan his escape and revenge.

Dark Visions

A violent twitch woke Prince Kendrick, Duke of Manshire. Initially, he could not determine if the impending crash in his nightmare or the venison pasty was the cause for the fire in his stomach. Queen Althea slept peacefully. She had had two of her favorite pasties and justified her choice as also eating for the baby.

Kendrick slid gently from under the covers; his toes found the floor's temperature to be cool and shivered from the cold air absorbed into his sweat soaked nightshirt. He sat on the edge of the bed rubbing his eyes before his trek to the kitchen.

Althea groaned. "Are you okay?" she asked. Her natural silky voice had a developing gravelly quality since the start of 'their' pregnancy—she sounded like a drunkard awakened outside a tavern.

"My stomach is burning. I am going to the kitchen for some milk," Kendrick replied. He rubbed his belly and tried to make sense of the nightmare's divergent images.

He finished the half goblet of milk and hunk of bread; the stomach fire was successfully extinguished.

While returning to the queen's chambers, he pondered the vivid nightmare images; *the magical appearance of the fifteen ballista siege machines, the bitter odor coming from the drawbridge area and the tall thin man with cropped white hair shaking his head while watching from inside the tree line. Kendrick wondered if he knew the man. The strangest image, however, was of a large man with long black hair, gathered in a ponytail, riding atop a black Clydesdale laughing as thousands of warriors oozed from the woods attacking the castle.*

Counter to the frightening nightmare, *a wonderful sensation of flying above the castle, ballista's and scurrying warriors made him feel invincible.*

Upon his return to the queen's chambers, he waited outside hoping for the collected intoxicating mix of extreme safety, ultimate power and blissful freedom to bless his mind, if only briefly.

Quietly he entered the room then closed the door. Tip-toeing in chambers, he prepared to slip silently into bed.

"How are you feeling?" asked Althea. "It is not like you to go to the kitchen."

"Sorry for waking you. I had a strange nightmare—more like a frightening vision which I observed while flying on a large bird," Kendrick replied. "But, the disturbing images are not fully connected."

"Maybe waking will break the nightmare's spell and pleasant dreams will follow."

"I hope your prediction is true."

Kendrick's eyes, though closed, did not aid in his sleep. After an hour of attempting to find a comfortable position, he finally slept.

Kendrick watched his reflection in the stale water, just west of the castle. He was a lad of fourteen. The intoxicating aura had returned and he did not care that he rode a great grey owl the size of a colt. Absorbed in the moment's pleasant mood, unaware of the arrows, he looked to the sky and watched as three black ribbons whisked toward the castle—the smaller ribbon wrapped around his chest. At that instant, he became fully aware of the battle below, that he had no weapons and was the target for many arrows.

The great owl flew at will—Kendrick could not alter the course—the ground ever closer now. An arrow struck Kendrick in the lung. He cried out in tremendous pain.

Suddenly the owl flapped franticly—a spear found its wing. Kendrick fell.

The owl flew away toward the west. Air rushed by as he fell the full height of the castle wall. His yell was silenced as the air rushed from his lungs when he slammed into the moat. Submerged, reflex triggered his throat to inhale. Water rushed into the vacant lungs, then his vocal cords swelled like wet leather choking off his throat. Darkness slowly constricted his vision until all was black.

>>><<<

"Kendrick, relax. Kendrick, wake up!" she shouted.

Attempting to hug his flailing arms proved to be unsuccessful. Althea ducked several arm swings and dodged a couple jabs. Her failed efforts to awaken him gave birth to thoughts that he might be in a trance. She rolled out of the bed, ran to the door, then grabbed the wash water pail.

Whoosh!—the water splashed his face, ran onto the floor and woke him. She placed the bucket on the floor.

"What happened?...Oh my!...*Flaming Dragons!*" Kendrick declared. He noticed the floor was wet around her feet. "Are we having a baby?" His chest heaved with every breath.

"No. But that might have been less dramatic than your nightmare," she replied. "Tell me about it."

"It was frightening. I felt possessed and could not wake." His breathing had calmed. "Something held me, forced me to see every image."

Kendrick's arms flapped as he told her about the great grey owl then his arms were still as he described the pleasure of flying. His smile distorted progressively to a frown when he revealed the black snake like ribbons, painful arrow in his lung, spear in the owl's wing and a helpless feeling of drowning.

->>><<<-

The edges of the two worn stone steps into the barracks held water when it rained. The weathered main door had turned grey from the morning sun. Oscar considered the steps and door functional, along with the interior walls that had water stains from the leaking roof and the three bunks declared unfit for use. Oscar had diverted the repair money to hiring three Long Bow Knights.

Kendrick knocked on Oscar's door.

"Come in."

"Good afternoon, Father."

Oscar's private room showed its age as well with four blocks of oak holding up one corner of the cot – one of the shutters held in place by a singular hinge.

"Good to see you. What brings you to the barracks?" Oscar asked.

"I have come to seek your guidance concerning a nightmare."

"Oh....a nightmare." Oscar focused on Kendrick's eyes expecting to see a hint of teasing. But he saw Kendrick's motionless tense face.

"Not just any nightmare, but a *frightening vision* like I have never experienced before," Kendrick said. Oscar directed Kendrick to sit on the cot and then moved to the edge of his chair.

"Describe your vision. I might be able to help, though it is a skill I have yet to master." For a few seconds, Oscar did not know what to do with his hands. His past belief in fate contradicted any potential for reliance on, or prophecy regarding dreams, nightmares and visions.

"I woke last night after part of the vision revealed the large bird I rode was crashing," Kendrick said while staring at the floor.

"How large?" Oscar asked—not sure where to direct Kendrick. He slid back into the chair and rocked it on the back legs.

"A great grey owl the size of a colt."

Oscar laughed, then instantly checked Kendrick's eyes. "I am sorry, the thought of an owl the size of a colt brought a humorous image to mind. Can you visualize those large feet attempting to catch small rodents?" Oscar was happy that Kendrick smiled. "A flying dream—those are delightful...usually. What did you find disturbing?"

"I counted fifteen siege machines aimed at the castle," Kendrick said. "And the air had a bitter smell originating from the drawbridge, but the owl would not fly by. I did see smoke."

"Ballista's?"

"Yes."

"Who could afford fifteen—maybe, three? They have to be moved for battle, maintained; and the supplies would be a

16

tremendous burden," Oscar said. "A bitter smell, like old wet oak or tar like?"

"Something I have never smelled before."

"I assume there is more?"

"A tall, thin man with white hair watched from the forest."

Oscar rubbed his beard. "He could be one of a thousand men in Manshire," Oscar, said as much to himself as Kendrick, looked past him. After a few seconds, he stared at Kendrick. "Sorry, you were saying?"

"Three black ribbons raced toward the castle then one separated and wrapped around my chest. My awareness of the danger I faced instantly replaced the euphoria of flying."

Kendrick had seen that look before—like a flying arrow, Oscar's mind went directly to target. Oscar set the chair's legs on the floor. He stood and paced.

"His hair, was it cut short and combed forward?" Oscar asked.

"Yes."

"Did he carry a long white walking stick?"

"Yes."

"Maybe fifty?"

"Yes. Who is he?"

Whole Recluse

Richard's rheumatism always flared up before any trip or long walk. At twenty-five the stiff hip and knee joints provided the first hints of a lifetime of pain and a family's curse as his sister had the same problem but her joint knots grew to the size of plums. Oscar had been understanding and loved Abbey deeply. Richard was thankful for that side of Oscar.

Abbey's brother, now forty-eight, envisioned himself as part mystic, part scholar and a whole recluse. He struggled with communication—he would wander off if the conversation did not suit his interest—another family curse that he had adjusted to for it gave him time to study.

He gathered his birch walking stick, the other toga and a knife for roots and berries. The two-day walk would clear his head and focus his mind on squelching Oscar's reaction. Richard guessed they would continue their *fate or free-will* debate until the queen interceded. He needed his wits sharper than dragons' teeth to convince the queen, Oscar and his nephew Kendrick of their bleak and devastating future.

>>><<<

Queen Althea was exhausted from the monthly meeting with her subjects—unprepared for the complaints over land ownership and crop retention—two multi-layered complex concepts that would require much discussion and consideration, which she planned to put off until a few months after the birth— maybe another less intricate matter would replace it.

When the room was empty she stood and stretched. She waddled like a duck to chambers with her hands pushing on her sore back.

Resting on her bed, every fiber of her body felt like the weight of large stones rested on her arms, legs and stomach restricting her movement. Yet a sense of obligation possessed her. She fell asleep within moments.

Standing next to a tall thin man with short hair, she watched as thousands of warriors followed groups of men carrying ladders across the fields toward the castle walls. As she started to leave, the white haired man thrust his birch walking stick in her path.

In stark contrast to her guide, a large, fat man with unruly black hair atop a large black Clydesdale horse rode a few feet in front of her. His saddle was a dark wolf hide. A bellowing laughter came from deep within emboldening the hard working warriors. The large crossbow machines continued to send large fire tipped arrows into a burning castle.

Aloft across the battlefield flew a large hawk diving and climbing. She felt pride, fear and compelled to watch the hawk. A moment later her fourteen year-old son, Madison and the hawk he rode were momentarily hidden by a forest of arrows. Ten arrows had pierced the hawk immobilizing its wings, uncontrollably gliding toward the moat. Althea emotionally felt water from the large loud splash. She leaned forward. Neither the son nor the hawk resurfaced.

Althea bolted from the forest toward the moat. While running she realized that the Long Bows were not shooting at the invaders—a few threw empty quivers at the advancing marauders. She was close to the moat when an arrow impaled the small of her back. She fell face first into the moat. Her legs were numb and her arms too short to lift her head above the waterline.

Althea's heavy erratic breathing woke Kendrick.

Abruptly she sat up in bed—a look of fear frozen on her face.

"Kendrick, hold me," Althea implored. They embraced for several quiet minutes.

"Are you okay?" Kendrick asked.

"Yes. But I had a devastating vision similar to yours. We must keep this between us. The queen cannot be known to have visions of disaster."

She told him of the influential laughing fat man, their young son riding a large hawk, many thousands of warriors, Manshire running out of arrows, helpless feeling while she drowned and the tall thin man.

->>><<<-

The next afternoon, Oscar took a deep breath, stared out the window and then faced Kendrick. "I knew this day would eventually arrive," he said in a soft tenor. He took a deep breath and released it in a light whistle. "Your mother had a brother. One summer we spent three very long days visiting your uncle Richard. She wanted to see him while she could walk. You were four."

Oscar glanced at the floor for a few moments. "Abbey had a gift. At the time I thought it was craziness. Now I am not so sure. Apparently, she could predict the future, or more accurately she could predict the outcome based on the choices available. She could see ribbons in the sky."

Kendrick interrupted, "I see ribbons occasionally."

"Well, your Uncle Richard, who claimed to have mastered the ability to read the ribbons, claimed that summer you had the gift and it was strong. Being a devout believer in *fate and destiny* I could not accept his *outcomes based on choices* and would not let Abbey discuss the gift with you. I feared that you would depend on someone, or something, that was not me, tarnishing my relationship with Richard."

"Wow." Kendrick wiped his hands through his hair as he looked to the ceiling.

"A morsel of advice from my narrow-mind, be open to *different* and do not deny your wife her family."

"I think since Althea is the queen..." Kendrick let the reply float away silently like driftwood. "How do you think this information fits into our visions?"

"Uncle Richard is a tall thin man with white hair combed forward to hide his balding. He walks with a long white birch stick—he has a milder version of the disease that crippled your mother. When you mentioned the black ribbon and the short white hair, I felt goose bumps travel up my spine. We should expect a visit from Richard."

Kendrick and Oscar flinched at the knock on the door.

"Captain. There is someone to see you," the sergeant said. "He said I should tell you to take your time, he had fourteen years."

"A tall white haired man that goes by Richard?" Kendrick asked.

"How did you know?" the sergeant replied.

Holding the door for Kendrick to exit the barracks, Oscar asked, "Where is he?"

"Sorry for the misunderstanding. He is waiting at the castle entrance," the sergeant replied.

Walking to the castle Kendrick rubbed his hands and fidgeted with his quiver.

"Why are you so nervous?" Oscar asked.

"I am uncertain," Kendrick replied.

"I should meet Richard alone."

"I will see you tonight at dinner?"

"Yes."

Kendrick turned toward the market and Oscar watched his son meld into the crowd, then continued to the main door.

Richard sat on the main steps leaning against the wall. "Good afternoon, Oscar." Facing the mid-June sun, his eyes remained closed.

"Good afternoon, Richard. Welcome to Manshire." He faced the sergeant, "Thank you. I can escort him from here."

"I half expected you would run me out of the village," Richard said.

"Maybe in my younger days. But, my son has taught me to be more accepting of different views and beliefs."

"I had prepared for an emotional challenge from you," Richard said. He smiled. "This is not a deceptive maneuver of some kind?"

"No deception. You can think of it as an apology for forbidding Abbey the freedom to visit her brother at will."

"Thank you, Oscar."

Oscar offered his hand to help him stand.

"What brings you to Manshire?" Oscar said shaking Richard's hand.

"Manshire's future is bleak and devastating."

Oscar stared at Richard. *He has been here maybe ten minutes and the words bleak and devastating are part of the conversation.* "How so?" he asked.

"Can we have this conversation in private with Queen Althea and Prince Kendrick?"

"I am again uncomfortable and prefer to hear what you have to say before making any introductions to Althea and Kendrick," Oscar said.

"Please, this one time, believe my intentions are noble. You can always describe me as a lunatic at the end."

Oscar scratched his head and stared at the steps for half a minute. "Come with me."

He asked the maids to leave the Assembly Hall and then turned his attention to Richard. "I will bring the queen and Kendrick here. I should be about ten minutes."

Oscar arrived with Kendrick and Althea to find Richard lying on the floor. He struggled to stand. "I have a joint disease and lying on the cool floor eases the pain."

Althea gasped and Kendrick covered his mouth with his hand—they looked to each other. "The tall man from my vision," the queen whispered.

"Same man from *my* vision," Kendrick added.

"Queen Althea, Kendrick, I introduce Richard, my brother-in-law. He has requested an audience with your grace to discuss what he calls a bleak and devastating future."

"This should be interesting," Althea whispered to Kendrick.

"Please be seated," Richard said. He waited for everyone to sit. "Your baby is the last opportunity to prevent the destruction of Manshire."

Kendrick, who was about to speak, noticed Oscar raise his hand to stop him.

"I am providing the following information for the purpose of validating my predictions and ability," Richard continued.

Kendrick leaned forward on the chair's arm. Althea pushed her chair back and sat on the front edge. Oscar leaned forward with his elbows on the table.

"In three days, your son will be a difficult delivery," Richard said. "He will die if the mid-wife's reaction to his sapphire complexion is slow. If he dies, Manshire will also die. The following morning his birthmark, a brownish oval discoloration will appear on his right shoulder."

Kendrick watched Richard furtively with narrowed eyes.

"You simply could be *lucky* with those predictions. If you have predictive abilities, will my son and I survive?" Althea asked.

Oscar turned quickly to assess Richard's reaction.

"The child will arrive when the moon passes the sun and a fleeting darkness covers Manshire. He will be the only brightness."

"When does our son become the last opportunity? If your predictions are true regarding the birth, can you provide the same clarity about the fate of Manshire as it relates to the baby?" Kendrick asked.

Oscar, surprised by Kendrick's reaction, wished he had taken their vision discussion more seriously.

"Fate will not determine the outcome. If it did we could only wait for Manshire to fall. There are scarce opportunities beforehand, but if they are missed, it will fall to him as the last resort. As to when, your son will be fourteen," Richard replied.

"Kendrick and I had similar visions of a vast army attacking and destroying Manshire. Images had similarities and differences. Do the differences represent the opportunities?" Althea asked.

"No. For Kendrick, they will be a quick sensation. For your son, the opportunities will be perceived as another learning experience—he will have no fear, which may place him in grave danger. For you, recognition will always be too late," Richard replied.

"What can you tell us about the *scarce* opportunities?" Oscar asked.

Richard smiled. "They are the result of decisions made by others along the way. Random and swift best describes their nature." Richard nodded to Oscar. "At this moment, here is what I can tell you about the last opportunity. Your recent past meets a

ANDEAN WHITE

powerful future. A false one becomes thousands. An ancient bird will perhaps save your son from the moat. Thousands of invaders will come from the east after traveling more than eight years.

Life's Dangers

Two days of worry interrupted Kendrick's sleep. Every movement that he considered abnormal resulted in waking Althea to ask if it was time. At four hours past dawn on day three of Richard's visit, Kendrick did not have to ask as Althea's first painful scream was unmistakable.

From the room next door, the portly mid-wife ran into the queen's chamber. "I apologize for my bed-clothes. I was certain the prediction was wrong and she had another month." She placed her hands on Althea's womb. "Do not push. Something is wrong."

"Is she going to be alright?" Kendrick asked.

"Please do not distract me." She continued to rub. Her wrinkled brow did little to comfort Kendrick.

The queen's chamber, the king's chamber of Althea's youth, was the largest bedroom. At this moment, it seemed small to Kendrick with three maids and Althea's natural mother, Samantha, standing and waiting for the birth.

Kendrick paced. The women wrinkled their noses and leaned back as he walked passed them. Samantha, usually the example of grace, held out her arm on his fourth pass. "Stop pacing," she whispered. "You are not helping Althea."

"I think your uncle might be right," said the mid-wife. "This baby is arriving early and going to be a difficult birth." She looked at Kendrick. "Why are you here?"

"Supporting my wife," Kendrick replied.

"A husband at the birth, this is a first for me. Have you delivered a baby before?"

"No." Kendrick focused on the floor and scratched the back of his neck. "I will be over here." He walked to the other side of the bed and held Althea's hand. He leaned near her ear, "You are going to be a great mother."

"*Ow!*" Althea yelled and squeezed his hand tightly.

"Don't push," the midwife said. "Sorry, but I need her undivided attention. Please leave the room. You can wait in the hall. And could you leave the…?" She pointed at his knife.

Kendrick placed his hand on the handle then tilted his head toward Samantha. She shrugged her shoulders.

He offered the handle to the mid-wife. "I will be outside in the hall," Kendrick said.

"I am counting on it," replied the mid-wife.

The door closed behind him. Oscar sat and cast his eyes toward the empty chair he had brought from the Assembly Room. "You lasted longer than I expected," Oscar said. "For future reference, birth is nature's magic and understood by women only. A man's place is waiting."

"Is Uncle Richard around?"

"He has such confidence in his abilities, he is probably still sleeping."

Kendrick sat then stared at his father for a moment. "I sense a deeper past feud then I originally thought," Kendrick said.

"Yes. Most of the tension between us came from my stubborn belief in fate."

A scream came from the queen's chambers. Oscar rested his hand on Kendrick's arm.

"If you trust Richard, the time to worry is when the moon passes the sun," Oscar said—he could not hide the tremor in his hand.

"Are you nervous?" Kendrick asked, squirming in the chair.

"Always, when things are outside my control and today—more than usual. For the first time I am placing my faith in Richard."

Kendrick leaned forward and lowered his head toward the floor before looking at Oscar. "Is there a part of you that hopes his predictions are wrong?"

"I cannot answer that question. If I say yes, I am continuing to belittle your mother's gift and refusing to use every resource to protect the kingdom. If I say no, then Manshire's survival may depend on sacrificing the unborn prince." Their eyes met momentarily, Kendrick smiled and Oscar winked. "Maybe it is fate that he arrived at this time."

A maid exited the room with an empty bucket. Kendrick was partially out of the chair when he glanced at Oscar who was shaking his head. Kendrick returned slowly to the chair.

"Not yet?" Kendrick asked.

"Not yet. You will hear the infant cry," Oscar replied.

Kendrick squirmed in the chair as he looked about. "Is it cloudy?" he asked.

"No. The sky was clear earlier. We have a few minutes, I would like to see the moon pass before the sun."

All of the nearby chambers were occupied. Walking fifteen feet through the hall, they passed the portrait of the former king.

Kendrick opened the hallway window to a strangely darkened world. The shadows around the fountain appeared to have shadows.

Oscar looked at the sun. An eye shaped dark portion slowly expanded across the surface. The faint shadows and the spaces between would soon be flooded in darkness.

"What is happening?" Kendrick asked.

"It is called an eclipse. The moon is passing between the earth and sun. It will last for another half hour," Richard said as he advanced from behind. "The prince will arrive in the next fifteen minutes."

A scream exploded through the quiet hallway. Kendrick knew from the battlefield that it was a scream of the wounded. Kendrick's instincts to stop the pain and protect his wife were fully engaged. He ran to the door and hurled it opened.

He heard his knife clank. With large eyes, Kendrick witnessed the boy being removed from the womb.

The mid-wife's hands were covered in blood as she handed the baby to Samantha and frantically sewed Althea's abdomen together.

Kendrick's thoughts were running wild in his head. *Is this a plot by Uncle Richard to get even with my father? This castle must be cursed. Why is she still bleeding?* He was about to address the mid-wife when the bleeding slowed.

Samantha, covered in blood, held a crying small baby. His arms and thighs were anemic.

The mid-wife breathed deeply then motioned for Kendrick to listen. She whispered in soft kind tones, "Talk to her about the handsome and healthy boy. Convince her all is well and she should rest."

He took her hand and felt a soft squeeze. "Althea, we are parents of a beautiful baby boy. He has strong lungs, your blue eyes and Oscar's small hands. You challenged the predicted complications in grand fashion, as I knew you would, you should rest now." He motioned to Samantha to bring the baby near. "Althea, open your eyes and gaze upon our son."

Althea looked at the now sleeping baby, smiled and mouthed *thank you.*

"My grandson will be a wonderful king," Samantha said.

"Althea, your mother will take care of the prince. I will be here for you."

The mid-wife pointed at herself.

"And the mid-wife will also be here," he said. Kendrick leaned close to her ear and whispered, "Althea, I love you."

The mid-wife smiled at Kendrick. The tension slowly drained from her face. With bloody hands and clothing, she turned to the chair. In moments she was asleep.

Kendrick greeted Althea instantly the three times she woke during the afternoon and night.

Althea's smile comforted him—Kendrick's smile seemed to give her strength.

An hour after sunrise, the mid-wife woke, stretched in the chair, stood, then stretched again. "I am sorry for sleeping, but knew you would wake me if needed." She walked to the bedside. "She will be sore for a week, but alive. I will watch her. You get some food and a nap." She washed her hands as Kendrick stood then she handed him his cleaned knife.

He reached for the door as it opened.

"Come outside," Samantha whispered, carefully turning the baby over. "Look at this. It was not there yesterday."

->>><<<-

Wandering through the rose garden Kendrick's mind skipped from thought to thought; the painful birth, Althea's fragile survival, the new birthmark and the anticipation of the other predictions. Uncle Richard had validated his ability.

Pressing his palms against the pounding ache behind his forehead, he looked down at the Amherst Roses—a few old buds from the late spring bloom giving their last ounce of fragrance. Darkness settled over the garden. Instantly Kendrick looked to the sky—a cloud moving across the sun had caught his attention.

In the third story window he saw his father smiling.

"An eclipse is rare and never comes in pairs," said Uncle Richard approaching from behind. "Did you see ribbons?"

"Yes."

"Their colors?"

"A small black and a full pink and blue. What does this mean?"

"The small black tells us a loved one is in danger. I believe that to be Althea. The pink ribbon predicts healing. Again Althea, but the color may include the repair of the relationship between Oscar and me. And the blue ribbon represents truth."

Kendrick pointed to the chairs made from stumps. "That is nice to know, but what makes it *useful.*"

"That will become evident later today when we discuss your son's role in saving Manshire. You are curious about your gift?"

"Yes, and how are you sure I have it?"

"You can see the ribbons and when you visited at a young age, splinters of sunlight illuminated two lines in a prophet's book you thumbed through in a moment of boredom."

Kendrick tilted his head. "I remember that book, closed with a clasp, blue, one of the few not covered with dust and hand printed."

29

"Excellent memory. That book was a gift from an old monk friend who travelled with a black wolf."

...from the lineage of the Queen's guard comes a lad with mystical powers whose father has unshakeable courage and willpower...

Kendrick's eyes opened wide when Richard handed him the book—it was old when he had read it twenty years ago. Could Bernard be the author?

"The ribbons confirmed my suspicion—two blue and two white for clarity and a new beginning."

A yellow strip of cotton marked a warning on the left page and the missing page on the right.

From a far darkness comes a fearless man riding a horse the color of midnight. Death and destruction follows him. Like bees his followers are loyal to the clan-like cause. They are well fed and intoxicated by the black power. A young child on an ancient bird...

The end of the prophecy was missing.

"Look to the sky. What color are the ribbons?"

Kendrick scanned the sky. "Two black, two violet and three indigo."

"Correct. Black warns of mourning, violet predicts incarceration and indigo indicates a foundation of deceit."

->>><<<-

A cloud of misfortune seemed to follow Bernyce. Her father had died hunting and her stepfather was a dreamer, which made him a bad provider. Two years ago the ramshackle farmhouse was swept away by a mudslide in what appeared to be her first bit of luck—she had been gathering firewood in the downpour.

At fourteen Bernyce wished to be average. Self-conscience and insecure about her diminutive size plagued her self-image—making her lonely and awkward socially. Working with the all male cathedral staff, she lacked the essential female example and a confidant needed by an adolescent girl. She had two dresses, the brown one for work and the blue one for church and other occasions.

Evenings were spent reading and studying in the cathedral library.

Respected by the staff as a dependable worker, she occasionally received jobs that filled her with joy and pride—a favorite being the flower gardens next to the cathedral walls.

Arrosa, a black and white spotted terrier, which she named in honor of her mother—the only person that showed her love and encouragement, had adopted her.

Then four days after the birth, Samantha began hinting to a weakened Althea, "Bernyce is smart, dependable, trustworthy and in need of a female mentor."

Two days later, Althea had proposed *nanny* Bernyce to Kendrick.

"I am not comfortable with her as a nanny. She could bring bad luck to our son," Kendrick had said.

"Kendrick, you and I have met every challenge and overcome dozens of potentially destructive situations." Althea had reached for his hand—her grip was strong.

"I will contact Bernyce this afternoon," Kendrick had said. "Have you given any thought to the prince's name?"

"I like Madison," Althea had said. A gleam in her eye and a smile told Kendrick he was about to concede to the queen's will.

"Madison it is."

->>><<<-

Kendrick found Quentin with the Archbishop planning the harvest blessing for Sunday.

"Gentlemen, I have come to ask permission to speak with Bernyce about becoming the prince's nanny," Kendrick said.

"*Ask permission*—do you think we would refuse? But, we have been expecting you."

"Uncle Richard predicted my arrival?"

"No. It was Althea," Quentin replied. "Bernyce is outside in the flower beds."

Kendrick smiled as he walked through the cathedral.

Red hair hung down from under a hand woven grass hat with a wide, flat brim and half round crown, which protected

Bernyce's fair skin. He watched her tilling the soil tenderly, pulling the weeds and watering with a ladle and bucket.

A spoon of water flew from the ladle.

"I am sorry for scaring you," Kendrick said.

"It is easy for me to forget my troubles when I work in the pretty flowers," Bernyce offered.

"I have come to ask if you would be interested in serving the queen by caring for our son."

"I will be at the castle tomorrow. The queen's maid talked with me yesterday."

"Look forward to seeing you then." He walked toward the castle's main entrance. He smiled, shook his head and walked a bit faster. He had been tricked by Althea and happy that she was feeling better. Regardless, he continued to have an uneasy feeling about Bernyce.

->>><<<-

Richard arrived at the barracks, entered and knocked on Oscar's door.

"Come in." Oscar sat on the floor repairing his cot.

Closing the door behind him, Richard asked, "The queen is alert and rested. I would like to complete my duty." He stared out the window then whispered, "This is the longest I have been away from home."

"Are you agreeable to a morning meeting tomorrow?" Oscar asked.

"Sure. Would you like some help? I am quite good at carpentry."

"Yes, if you have the time," Oscar teased.

"Pass the chisel."

Richard leaned on one knee, held the tenon of the new cot leg against the floor, then slowly shaved several slivers.

"I feel a need to say this, but I am sure you have thought about the long range planning. Manshire will never have the military might to defend against the vast marauder hordes," Richard said.

Oscar pointed to a flat spot on the cot leg. "Shave a little from each side." He handed the leg to Richard. "I agree. I am curious; do you have a sense of why marauders from the east would be interested in little Manshire? We do not have any minerals, precious metals, climate...." He turned his head away from Richard and coughed—the cough reverberated deep inside his chest.

Richard patted between Oscar's shoulder blades. "Your progress will be slow. You might die from an event associated with your duties before the illness takes your life." He gave the cot leg to Oscar.

"It fits. Nice work," Oscar said. "We will meet in the queen's chambers. The mid-wife wants Althea to stay off the stairs for a few more days."

"Until tomorrow."

->>><<<-

When Richard, Oscar and Kendrick arrived the mid-wife and Bernyce left the room.

"Your birth predictions proved to be accurate. What is the rest of the prophecy?" asked Queen Althea.

"The marauder hordes will arrive at the next eclipse in fourteen years. After the leader has formed his vast army an enemy from Manshire's past will deceive him. The last opportunity for Manshire's survival rests on the shoulders of an ancient bird ridden by Madison."

Kendrick and Althea exchanged glances. "How did you know we named our son Madison?"

"It was part of my vision," Richard said. "The marauders will be powerfully motivated and extremely dangerous when they discover the false one has lied to them. Also, after the crest of the eclipse, be warned that the horde will take things into their own hands if their leader is absent for even a short time."

The next morning Richard left at dawn without a good-bye, but stopped momentarily to wave at Kendrick watching him exit the castle. He tugged twice on the white portion of his toga then brushed his hand across the sky. Kendrick saw the white ribbons and knew from the garden meeting with Richard it was a new beginning, but was not sure if it was a good one.

Long Range

Queen Althea's had delayed Oscar's request until her health returned. She suspected they would talk about a single item, Madison flying a large bird.

She watched as he furrowed his brow, saw his lips move as if he were practicing and was sure she would grow dizzy if he did not stop pacing.

"Queen Althea, Prince Kendrick, I am forty-three and do not think I will make it another fourteen years," Oscar said. "We need to get my replacement trained."

She covered a short gasp. Oscar had always been near—rescuing, protecting and advising her.

"I could refuse to accept your retirement as your queen," she said, spacing out the words. What could she do to change the inevitable? Her voice quivered at the thought of life without Oscar. "But it would only waste valuable preparation time."

"I suspect you have a plan," Kendrick said—shaking his head slowly while looking at the floor.

Oscar smiled at his son.

I am fighting back tears and these two are worried about the job—Althea thought.

"Yes. I suggest Zachary become what traditionally has been the Captain of the Guard. And, we develop a special skills squad of ten knights led by the sergeant. Both men are qualified for their new responsibilities—Zachary is very good with the knights and has a good, tactical mind. The new group would be assigned delicate covert tasks. The sergeant follows orders regardless of the consequences and finds a way to complete the assignment."

Rubbing a palm with his thumb, he waited a few moments. "We do not need to decide today, but soon."

The queen stood, walked across the room, momentarily stared at the wall and then quickly turned toward Oscar. "Have you developed some initial plans for saving Madison and Manshire?" She realized the implication of her question and set her gaze toward Kendrick.

"Some basic schemes that do not depend on Madison and *a large bird*—hiding army soldiers and weapons outside and inside the castle. Evacuating the village to entrap the enemy. Add new defensive tools on the walls. Disable the drawbridge. And, we may need to plan the destruction of the castle to save Manshire," Oscar replied. "But, I suspect better schemes to come from meetings with Kendrick."

->>><<<-

Summers were spent outside gathering fruits and berries, tending the gardens, repairing the cathedral and caring for the animals—no class work. For Luxton these types of lessons had more value than studying why two women turned to salt. His blisters, splinters and cuts had purpose—he had completed meaningful work. And, he was getting stronger—maybe by summer's end he would have the strength to challenge Ulster.

After dinner and during the shuffle of dishes, which were returned to the kitchen, Luxton would vanish under the sheets to the boys' washroom to clean the dirt from his neck and cool his red sun soaked skin.

The washroom was an odd assortment of twenty water buckets setting on wooden crates collected from clothing donations. Donated clothes too big for the children were arranged carefully across the back of the buckets in an attempt to keep them dry. Draped over the bucket's front edge was the rag for washing away the grime from today's labor.

For five minutes he would be alone enjoying the healing water. Today was special for Luxton, he grinned as he examined the bucket the old handyman had let him build on his own.

He felt safe in the washroom—it was a location Ulster never used simultaneously with the children. Standing by his bucket the small rag was dipped and wrung out. Luxton closed his eyes and bowed his head then slowly cleaned the back of his neck.

Leaning over the bucket he buried his sun burned face into the now soaked rag. He smiled as the cool water relieved the sting and wished for a solution that would stop the beatings.

Conflicting options clouded his thoughts of running away. He would have to face fear alone, but he would not have to worry about Head Master Ulster. *Ideally, if I had the old handyman's job—a variety of work, very little communication with Ulster, free room and free food—the job would be ideal.*

The first footsteps of the boys approaching the washroom created a small panic within his heart. Soon it would be a beehive.

I could clean the barn, milk the cows and tend the garden. But, another boy, the old handyman, or myself completed these tasks now. Why would Ulster 'hire' me? He gets these chores completed for free. Luxton concluded that the only difference between the handyman and himself was that the handyman had never been beaten.

He rinsed the rag and replaced it on the buckets edge—closed his eyes, took a deep breath and smiled.

An unexpected splash and clanking sound startled him. He twisted as a bucket flew toward his head.

Luxton expelled every breath of air from his lungs. His hands quickly reached to protect the bleeding ear and the lump forming on the back of his head—another strike might kill him.

->>><<<-

Time moved slowly for Ulster as Luxton exhaled. He prepared to strike again. Their eyes locked, but Luxton's hands were too slow to provide protection as the bucket again struck the orphan—this time squarely on the forehead.

Ulster did not have time to clean the blood from the bucket or the floor. He replaced the bucket, pulled on Luxton's arms and slipped away from the washroom. The trail of water would dry before anyone determined Luxton was gone.

After everyone had gone to bed, Ulster returned to the wine cellar. Luxton's bruised body lay unrestrained on the floor.

Ulster put on the bloody goat skinned glove and knelt beside Luxton's bloody face.

"I have been unable to control the behavior of you trouble-makers. Now your mysterious disappearance will seed enough doubt that no one will challenge me."

Ulster poked Luxton's bleeding and puffy face. His right eye had swelled shut and the left opened to a tiny slit. Luxton attempted to scream when Ulster touched his jaw.

"Your paltry whimper will not be heard by anyone," he said. "You and I are taking a short wagon ride." He pressed Luxton's broken ribs. "If you survive, do not return, or I will surely slay you."

Ulster pulled Luxton to a sitting position, lifted him onto his shoulder, walked ten feet and dropped him on the wagon bed. He smiled at the boy's worthless groan.

They traveled for thirty minutes before Ulster stopped, walked to the back of the wagon, gripped Luxton's feet and pulled him until he fell on the ground. Without a word Ulster slapped the reins and turned the wagon toward the cathedral.

Now he was ready for the Archbishop's visit.

->>><<<-

Bernyce continued to impress Althea and Kendrick. At two months Madison's cheeks were puffy and his upper arms and thighs were plump. There were no signs he had been delivered early.

At three months Madison's smiles were the center of castle conversations. Many of the staff passed the Queen's chambers to hear him say, "flada", "atha", or "kadak". Oscar had made a wooden mobile with stars, rings and moons that he enjoyed with Madison each day he was in the castle.

Bernyce showed the first signs of frustration at five months as Madison kept removing his shoes. Kendrick and Althea played peek-a-boo each night before bed, though a couple of months later Bernyce had had to childproof the Queen's quarters—Madison was crawling and chewing every object he could fit in his mouth. One month later she had to move the same items higher as Madison was walking.

When Madison turned nine months and he looked normal, Bernyce stopped her fanatical quarantining when she heard a cough or witnessed a fever. She seemed to have a sixth sense about what Madison needed for a healthy body. Her new focus was improving Madison's sleep. Since birth he never slept or napped longer than two hours. Part of her obsession included Kendrick and Althea reading to Madison. When Bernyce could not find a suitable book, she wrote short scripts for them to perform.

A month before Madison's first birthday he displayed symptoms of a cold, his nose dripped, his body was hot and his breathing became raspy. In the past four months, lung fever had infected twenty-six people; sixteen children under five years old had died.

->>><<<-

He ached everywhere.

Small lightning bolts rippled pain throughout his face and neck with every raindrop.

"I cannot lift my arms," he tried to say. Panic replaced his soul—*do I have arms? I have no feeling from my hands.*

He was confused. Nothing made sense. Had Ulster given Luxton's soul to the devil? No matter—Luxton swore...

After ten minutes pain returned to his arms, small movements required his full effort. On his back, he lifted his knees. Raising his arm then leaning his knees toward the road he rolled to his side. Repeatedly pushing with his arms for a moment, then resting for several seconds finally brought him to a kneeling position.

Using his left hand to hold open his left lid, he scanned his right hand and arm. Blood stained his clothing. His broken little finger pointed away from the palm.

He looked for cover from the rain.

Fifteen minutes of slow, agonizing crawling finally placed him against a pear tree.

The tree directed water down the trunk into a pool contained by rocks and large roots. He was frightened by the reflection of his once pleasant round face now covered in welts and cuts. His teeth looked like a checkerboard as two were missing on the top and three from the bottom.

He rested against the trunk.

Luxton swore...revenge.

->>><<<-

The last flickering sliver of sun which disappeared beyond the horizon produced brief, pleasant sunsets. Bernyce held Madison's hand as they crossed the hall to view the spectacular display.

Five minutes later Althea and Kendrick would arrive to read to him.

"Welcome," Bernyce said. She had continued to bow even after the Queen had given her an exemption.

"Good evening, Bernyce," Althea said.

"What book have you selected for Madison tonight?" Kendrick asked.

"I finished a short story yesterday about a boy and his dog," Bernyce replied. "Madison likes my dog, Arrosa and he is the only one she never barks at. I think Madison has visual commands for Arrosa. Yesterday he waved his arm and she ran around the room following his hand."

"We enjoy the stories you write and think Madison is more attentive when we read them," Althea commented.

"I'll be back in half an hour." She was fifteen feet down the hall when she remembered her towel and soap.

She heard Kendrick pick up the pages and sit. "In a great country lived a young Richard and his dog Heaven..."

Bernyce stopped at the door to listen to her story.

"...Heaven licked Richard's face," Althea said. She had taken the book from Kendrick, but Madison was already peacefully asleep. She laid the last page on the chair.

Through the gap created by the door's hinges, Bernyce could see Althea and Kendrick holding hands while they watched Madison.

"We have a wonderful son," Kendrick said.

"How true. We have also been blessed with an exceptional nanny. Bernyce continues to do a little extra. It is always a pleasure to see her finish a project because a pleasant surprise is coming. Last week she changed the crib blankets on her own."

"I thought you had one of the chambermaids do that because Bernyce was too short."

"Well, in typical Bernyce style, she had that step made." Althea pointed at the white box aside the crib. "Now she does not have to find someone to help her get Madison from the crib."

"It is nice to work with a self driven dependable person. She reminds me of my father," Kendrick said.

"Yes. How true. She challenged that fox last month in the rose garden. When I heard the story it was easy to visualize her tenacity. I felt sympathy for the fox."

"I have witnessed her reading in the cathedral library at night after we have read to Madison," Kendrick said.

"Should we arrange a guard?" Althea replied. "What is she doing in the library that late?"

Bernyce turned and walked to her room to wash.

Of Sisters and Horses

"We might be marking a new event for Manshire Castle—a normal royal birth," Oscar said.

"I find that hard to believe," Kendrick replied.

"At least in my time. Queen Francine had four stillborn boys. Then Althea was exchanged for another aborted boy. Come to think of it, Quentin was a regular birth, but the queen died from an infection. Madison's birth was a miracle—he was pre-mature and Althea survived caesarian surgery."

"Do you think Manshire is cursed?" Kendrick whispered, trying not to wake Madison.

"The four boys died from a poisonous type of tea the queen drank to ease the pain. Without the fatal brew, one or all may have lived," Oscar said. "Son, if this was a troubled birth, Richard would be here." *Or if the birth or death was significant to the looming invasion.*

Kendrick stared into the sky as he mindlessly stroked the sleeping Madison's hair.

"Strangely, today is the third month and third day after Madison's third birthday. Maybe three will be our new good luck number," Kendrick said. His confident smile had returned. "Today is going to be good, the two ribbons are white. They forecast a new beginning and so far nothing bad has happened on white days."

The rose garden was silent. Oscar and Kendrick looked to the window of the queen's chambers.

"Kendrick, I have been thinking that spending time with Uncle Richard might be helpful. We should look to everything that may contribute to our victory in eleven years," Oscar said.

"I have had similar thoughts. Do you think a week is enough?"

"When you returned with Abbey he said to her a month would be enough. That probably translates to two weeks of steady concentrated work," Oscar said.

"About the grand battle we face in eleven years, I want to discuss a tactic that keeps recurring..."

At that instant a maid entered the rose garden. "It is a healthy girl. The birth was uneventful."

Kendrick woke Madison. "You have a baby sister."

"Ith her arrided?" Madison said in his best baby talk. He smiled.

"Yes, she has arrived. Want to meet her?"

"Yeth!" Madison grabbed Kendrick's index finger and tugged. "Huree, fath."

Kendrick looked to Oscar. "Ready?"

"Yeth!"

->>><<<-

Luxton's appearance kept him hungry.

For six days the foul tasting pears dropping on the ground had saved his life. Begging in the villages involved screaming women and children when they saw his face. Most men walked around him. A few times he was chased away by a cluster of shop owners.

He became a nocturnal creature raiding gardens and fields—though food was easier to gather, it was of limited selection. Winter forced him to raid barns for raw eggs, stored potatoes and chickens. He hated chicken more than pears. Rabbits and rats were hard to catch and foods he preferred to avoid.

For two years he quietly roamed the farms, but three months ago he was frightened by a band of armed farmers yelling for *Malus* to leave. Luxton's bad luck had followed him to another farming region.

He climbed a tree to sleep safely above predators. He cried. Ulster had destroyed his life to save the job, which the Head

Master hated. In fits of rage Ulster had taken his frustrations out on him—many times.

He let the tears drip off his horribly disfigured face.

Fatigue and frustration ripped through his body with the speed of a fox racing through a chicken coop. He worried about farmers finding him, but only for a few minutes until he slept—another opportunity to dream of a better place.

He was walking a city street followed by a boy named Troy and fifty orphaned boys. A turkey leg in one hand and a sword in the other swung freely as he walked. Luxton's stomach was full, his head held high though citizens looked away as he passed. He arrived at the town square. The dead bodies of the clergy lay against the wheels before being loaded into the wagon.

A moment of peace calmed his heart and breathing when he saw the fire pit surrounded by a square of large pine logs.

Abruptly, Ulster raced toward him from two shrubs. His new friend Troy yelled, "Malus. Behind you!" Luxton spun with the sword extended fully. Ulster stopped and squatted as the sword passed over his head. Ulster slapped Luxton, "You can never be rid of me."

Luxton was frightened from sleep. Sweat dripped off his face. Wiping his face as he looked to the south he saw the lights of the city. *There is nothing left here for me. Maybe the city will be easier—a new start and I can put forth a fearless attitude.*

And maybe a new name? Everything bad has happened to me as Luxton—I would be fearless and feared in the city.

Rain started as he left the tree and within two miles he was slopping in three inches of mud. The drops pelted the top of his head, dripped off his eyelids, fell from the tip of his nose and ran down his neck.

Anger simmered as he pondered why Ulster had abused him. Could he simply have been a scapegoat? *I showed a tolerance for pain and he only had to worry about revenge from me. As long as Ulster could control the strongest orphan the other boys feared him. Why did he dispose of me like wash water? Was I of no value even to Ulster?*

His ears were hot despite the cold wind.

Why had the Archbishop let the beatings continue? Perhaps he did not know of such things. *No excuse! The archbishop was responsible to know. How did he miss the bruises on my legs and arms? He inspected us at the start of each visit. He walked through the dining hall as we ate.*

The former orphan could feel his face turning crimson. Anger purified his tired soul. The two men who should have had a positive and significant impact on his life either abused him or simply ignored the situation. They must be stopped!

He dared the rain to challenge his spirit. A cold north wind blew from behind. As Luxton, he would have looked for a dry place. He smiled. *I will never be weak again as...*Malus!

->>><<<-

On the fifth day since the princess's birth, Kendrick and Madison arrived at the Queen's quarters after morning meal. Bernyce was humming a lullaby and rocking the baby as they entered. Althea was facing out the window with her eyes closed.

"Enjoying the sun?" Kendrick asked.

"Yes. Good morning," she replied. "And good morning to my favorite prince."

Madison swallowed a couple times, tilted his head and stared into Althea's eyes. "Hello, mother. How ith the printheth?" he said in his best speaking voice.

"She is wonderful today." Althea glanced at Kendrick. "Oscar was here and he left this carved angel necklace for our daughter. Have you decided on a name for the princess? It has been four days."

"I like Eileen or Catherine," Kendrick replied.

"What do you think of Guinevere?"

"Babeeth do not aribe whith naymth?"

Althea and Kendrick grinned.

"Do you have a suggestion?" Althea asked Madison.

"I like Rothlyn. The tholdier frum the poemtry," Madison replied.

Kendrick looked to Bernyce.

"Roslyn was a shy child that grew up to lead a small group of soldiers in a battle against hundreds of marauders. The title of the poem was Lovely Rose," Bernyce replied.

"I like Roslyn," Althea said.

"Madison. Good choice." Kendrick put his arm on his son's shoulder.

"Thenk yoo," Madison replied. "Wheer ith Arrosa?"

"I do not know. She is usually here to greet you every morning," Bernyce said.

Through the window, Kendrick faintly heard Arrosa's playful bark, which usually meant she was with the horses.

"Althea, I will help Madison look for Arrosa."

"I have a meeting with the ministers," Althea said with a slight grin.

"If you finish early, you can help us look," he whispered, knowing the truth. There were no ministers meetings today.

Kendrick walked toward the stables, enjoying the morning and giving Madison time to run along the street; stopping frequently to check rocks, pinecones and needles under the trees.

Unfortunately, before they reached the stables, yells were heard from more than one man and the hooves of a bucking horse were clapping the stone street. Kendrick ran to Madison then carried him around the corner as the bucking horse kicked its vulnerable owner underneath. Blood dripped from his hair as he tried to avoid contact with another front hoof.

"Madison. Stay by this shrub." Kendrick waved a stable boy over to watch his son.

Kendrick's attempts to control the horse by grabbing the reins were unsuccessful, as they were tied together over the mane. The horse paused and shook his head, slinging slobber on Kendrick's palm. He grasped the shortened leather straps before taking a quick glance to see that Madison was safe, but he was not by the shrub. The stable boy was franticly searching for Madison. Kendrick scanned the street for his son, but could not find him. His heart pumped wildly.

In that instant the horse bucked, pulled the reins from Kendrick's slimy hand and kicked him in the shoulder. He stumbled backwards for three large awkward steps—his heel tripping on a stone and his head smacking against the stone street.

Kendrick, though dazed, called to Madison while attempting to stand unsuccessfully. Woozy, he checked the area, but it was too late! He could only watch as his son raised his hands in a V pattern and stepped in front of the mad horse. "Still. Peace. Rest," Madison said. His voice was calm.

Kendrick promptly extended his head toward Madison. *Did I hear Madison's voice without the childhood imperfections?*

The black horse towered over the child prince as it raised up on its back legs, shook its head, then lowered his long nose to Madison's outstretched hand. His son continued to whisper, "Still. Peace. Rest."

"Petting the white spot between the large nostrils he asked, "What is the matter?" A quick snort followed by a spirited neigh— the only sound in the stable area.

"A thorn on your knee?"

He walked to the side and placed his small hand against the powerful front leg. Gently, Madison rubbed the fold on the back of the knee upward against the lie of the hair. With his forefinger and thumb and drool dripping from the horse, he manipulated the thorn out of the hair.

Several small groups had gathered around whispering and pointing at Madison.

Kendrick stumbled to his feet and offered the horse's owner a hand.

"Did you see that?" the owner asked.

"Yes," Kendrick replied. Alternating his glance between Madison and the horse, Kendrick crouched while approaching Madison. His mind debated whether to scold him for not staying by the shrub, or hug him for an amazing demonstration.

"Where did you learn to do that?"

"Be brade ith in the poemtry about Rothlyn," Madison said.

Kendrick was surprised by the calm of Madison's voice. The murmur of the crowd tickled Kendrick's awareness. He glanced at the witnesses of his young son calming a thousand pound horse.

Arrosa was running out of the stables toward them. She arrived and sat calmly by the horse.

"Son, we should take the dog to Bernyce," Kendrick said, wanting to escape the growing crowd.

Madison pointed and Arrosa walked to the castle door.

Kendrick looked back at the calm horse, then at his son and finally to the window where Althea and Bernyce were talking. *I must find the poem* Lovely Rose.

Another Kind of Orphanage

Early morning, Malus walked the outskirts of Vlada. The storm clouds dissipated into thin wisps that reminded him of campfire smoke.

From the hilltop Malus could see where five villages had grown together along the river and the ocean shore. The land surrounding the northern part of the city was flat and fertile and partitioned into ten and twenty acre fields. The tenant farmers lived in ramshackle huts in the corners of the fields.

Gradually the streets filled with people. He walked under an apple tree, picked one and took a big bite. Fifteen minutes later he observed twenty carts filled with fruits, vegetables, meats, clothing and toys setting-up along the streets.

The handcart drivers argued about imaginary lines and raced other merchants for corner spaces.

Malus believed he had finally been blessed with abundance. The handcarts had every item he could ever need. An hour later more carts arrived with bread, jams, jellies, bedding, knives and kitchen tools. *This must be what a marketplace looks like.*

After thirty minutes, the bargaining hum rose as shoppers arrived. Malus kept his face down, covered his eyes like he was blocking the sun to better hide himself and moved slowly toward the merchant selling hats and gloves.

The hat merchant seemed to be interested in the buyer at the next cart selling bread. Three ladies were trying hats for size and function. As a shopper walked between the merchant and Malus, he slipped a black hat from the cart and walked away slowly. At another cart he grabbed an apple, at yet another, sundried meat found its way into his hand.

Malus left the market area and dunked the hat in the nearest rain puddle. The water would age the hat and stretch it to fit his head.

He explored more of Vlada's outer neighborhoods looking for places to hide with ample food supplies. *Those merchants have to purchase their goods somewhere.* Malus completed his surveillance of the north side then hid on the edge of the estuary in trees with knee high bare roots.

He removed his shoes when the tide started to rise. An hour after sunset, the water was up to his ankles and the bridge had only three travelers. With his hat covering most of his face, he walked across in bare feet. After wiping his feet on a patch of grass and rubbing sand from the top of his foot, he put on his shoes and looked for a place to rest.

Malus wandered into a vineyard and searched under the large leaves hoping to find ripe grapes. The barking from two dogs grew louder as he ran to the end of the row and turned south onto a dirt trail. He was not sure how long he could outrun the dogs, they were barking mercilessly; luckily they chased him for only another hundred yards.

The rolling hills of the river's south bank were rich with volcanic ash and minerals—excellent for producing grapes, olives, nuts, tobacco and tea leaves.

He walked a street with four warehouses, the smell of decaying fruits and vegetables refreshing bad memories of cleaning the orphanage kitchen and the offensive odor from weeks of old fruit, vegetable skins and rinds in the garbage pit. Tomorrow he would return to discover the best times to find food.

He walked a couple miles before coming upon an abandoned barn surrounded by unkempt grass, weeds and vines. Slowly scouting the area for over protective farmers or their dogs, he found a well-worn path to the backside.

Malus hid behind a hedge eighty feet from the barn door hoping he had found a place to sleep and was surprised five minutes later when eight boys left the barn. They reminded him of the orphanage misfits as they bumped and shoved each other while scanning, the area, Malus was sure to avoid detection. He followed them to the four warehouses where they crouched next to a rock wall.

Two men unloaded a wagon of wooden boxes marked *Apples* and in smaller letters at the bottom *One Peck*. Malus watched as a man exited the warehouse and begin hauling the boxes inside. When, what Malus assumed was Mr. Peck, had been gone for about thirty seconds, the boys ran to the crates. One scouted while the other scoundrels stole four or five apples apiece. They ran back to the wall.

A minute later the warehouseman returned, shook his fist in the air and shouted, "I will get you for stealing my apples!" Mr. Peck tossed apples from one box to another. He seemed concerned about the boxes looking the same. After the apple-swapping event, he picked up another box and disappeared through the door.

The boys ran in the direction of the barn, their worn shoes taking them away from the angry Mr. Peck armed with a pitchfork.

With his new name, Malus followed the pitchfork. He would stop every angry adult abusing a child and his new name would give him the courage he needed.

The boys had split up into four pairs and Mr. Peck had stopped momentarily, appearing to decide which pair to follow. He sprinted to his right toward a fallen boy whose partner had left him.

"Stop!" Malus ran up the trail through the weeds at Mr. Peck who had lifted the fork above the boy's head. A moment later he was twenty feet to the pitchfork that was aimed at him—Malus alternated glances at the edges of the path and the sharp weapon. At ten feet Malus jumped to his right hoping his foot found the short stump. He watched the worn tangs of the pitchfork as they were thrust out at his former location. Malus's quick maneuver compelled Mr. Peck to step forward or the combined weight of the pitchfork and his violent thrust would cause him to fall. Malus's fist struck the side of Peck's neck. Upon landing he turned then punched Mr. Peck in the lower back causing him to fall to his knees. The man moaned in pain.

Malus offered his hand to the boy. "What is your name?" But, the boy kept his eyes on Mr. Peck gasping for air.

When he had found his balance he looked into Malus's eyes. "Oh my! What happened to your face! Never mind, I do not want to know. My name is Troy. Friends call me Troyboy. What is your name?"

"Malus."

"Strange name."

"It is Latin for ugly or wicked."

Mr. Peck grunted and hobbled away.

"Sorry. Well Malus, I am very happy to meet you. Come and I will introduce you to our little group and Lord Randolf." Troy skipped and spun on the trail while talking and stared at Malus's face when he walked backwards. "Where did you come from? Do you know Randolf? Thanks for saving me." He tossed an apple to Malus. "Here, these are good in the fall. How did your face get so scary?"

"The head master beat me." *Luxton's* body shook and his knees buckled slightly as he remembered the pain of Ulster's beating and the insults shouted into his bloody ears. A few seconds passed before *Malus* remembered his promise to never be afraid again.

"That happens a lot. Most of Lord Randolf's army have scars received at an orphanage," Troy said.

At the barn's field, Troy stopped then knelt in the overgrown weeds and grass. "We wait here until everyone returns."

"We are all here plus one too many," said a boy. "Randolf will not like this."

"I could not leave him. He saved my life," Troy said.

As they entered the barn, flashbacks of the orphanage caused trembling within Malus's body. He looked up. Sheets hanging from ropes cordoned off Lord Randolf's room. Each boy's bed was a thin square of straw sprinkled on the ground. He guessed thirty *beds*. It appeared they shared a single wash bucket.

"And who are you?" a husky, short man, barked. A cloud of dust developed when he slapped his chest. *Is this Lord Randolf?*

I must show no fear. Malus slowly pushed his shoulders back and stared into the short man's eyes.

Randolf's head jerked back as he said, "You are the ugliest person I have ever seen."

No matter. "I would be happy to add you to the top of that list," Malus said fearlessly.

Whispered mumblings sprouted among the wide-eyed boys. Troy's face turned ashen as he looked disgustedly at the *ex-friend* that had saved his life.

Malus winked at Troy.

"No, no. I should have asked what happened to you. I apologize," Randolf said.

Malus heard the tremor in his voice and grew concerned. Was this just another type of *orphanage?*

->>><<<-

Kendrick entered the Queen's chambers.

"Calming the horse was unbelievable," Althea said. She knelt with arms open wide to hug Madison.

"Yes, and I think he can do it at will," Kendrick whispered. "Arrosa responds to Madison's visual commands."

Althea looked to Bernyce who had offered her hand to Madison.

"Would you like to draw?" she asked as they exited the room.

"Yeth, that would be fun," Madison replied.

Althea waited for the door to close.

"I have not been ready to talk about our son's future because I want him to remain a young boy. It might be foolhardy, but I fear when this discussion is over I may have to visualize him only as a battle soldier." Biting her lower lip, she stared at the fire for a moment before she paced her chambers as though a path had been created for her—walking along the outer wall, around the hearth, passed the bed, then back to the starting point.

"Our previous discussions have stalled because we had more questions than answers within Richard's prophecies and our visions," Kendrick said. "We could surrender and take…"

"No! We are not surrendering," Althea interrupted. She noticed Kendrick's quick, sly grin. "We could train someone to take Madison's place."

She had made a complete lap. "As tempting as that sounds for Madison, we put another family in the same troubling decisions as we are facing. And, the invasion would eventually become public knowledge. I would suggest a prisoner, but they would fly away."

Kendrick concentrated on the floor and walked with his hands behind his back, keeping to the opposite side of the circular path. "We could dress Madison in armor."

"I had thought about armor, but I cannot get his drowning out of my mind. Perhaps that is why Madison drowns in my vision?"

"We can assemble a standing, or temporary army," Kendrick suggested, knowing there was not enough men in Manshire to build a force that could stop thousands of marauders. He stopped at the window—three black ribbons—death!

Althea stopped to face Kendrick. "We are farmers, which begs the question, 'what are the marauders' interests in Manshire?' We do not have an abundance of minerals or wealth?" She rubbed her temples, closed her eyes and swayed slowly. After a minute she continued, "Besides, the temporary army we assembled to fight Argo, was a ruse to keep him and Cromwell occupied. If our army had been a fighting force, we would have attacked."

"How about a different approach—Madison commands the bird with hand signals within a protective band of Long Bows?

Althea placed her hands on the back of her neck and stared thoughtfully at the ceiling. "What is the bird's function in this battle? In our visions, Madison, or you as Madison, flew about on various large birds. What do birds do that can change the outcome of an invasion? They fly, build nests, lay eggs, feed young...forage for food, search for predators and attack to protect young."

"Perhaps our son should only survey and tell us when and where to strike," Kendrick replied. He rubbed his forehead with his fingertips, breathing deeply. *Something is not right with our thinking.* "We are back at the same void. A visit to Richard is required. He may not be the source we need, but the information might be in Richard's disorganized library."

She stopped at the bed, sat on the mattress and leaned on her hands, gripping the blankets. "Another vague meeting with Richard," she said in a low voice, shaking her head.

Kendrick walked to the window. On the eastern horizon, drifting across the clear soft blue sky, were two dark blue ribbons. From that day in the rose garden with Richard, was it a new beginning? No...something, like...clarity—that was it.

Kendrick waved to Bernyce as she entered the castle's side door, which was directly across from the cathedral's library entrance.

As he entered the cathedral library for only the third time in his life, he looked at the oak timber floor and squeezed the back of his neck.

"Where can I find the poem *Lovely Rose*?" Kendrick asked as the young librarian approached.

"Sir, you are the third person to ask in the last week," the priest said. "It is our only copy, which was returned yesterday."

"By whom?"

"Queen Althea and Captain Oscar. Follow me, sir. The book is in the next aisle."

The prevalent dust on the adjacent books helped mark the book of poems, which had been cleaned for the queen. The priest removed the book and handed it to Kendrick. "The best light is over there." He pointed to the table under a small stained glass window.

Thumbing through the book he found two dog-eared pages—*Lovely Rose* and *Angelic Ghosts*. *Lovely Rose*'s bent triangle was dirty from fingers rubbing against it. But the *Angelic Ghosts* marker was clean. He read Roslyn's poem.

ANDEAN WHITE
Lovely Rose

Summer crusades
Marauders made,
Farmland stained
Buried sons remain.

An advancing giant
Attacked from within,
By slightest knight
And fold of ten.

Doubtful tho't team,
Of girl's fresh scheme.
So swiftly they moved—
Roslyn theory approved.

A gardener's offspring,
Legendary bravery told—
Battles with mighty sting,
From life of lovely rose.

"Yes!" Kendrick shouted.
He was sufficiently shushed by the young priest.
"Sorry."

He read it again, his heart beating with the strength of a bull. Kendrick felt invincible; the words had left the page and were branded within his brain.

He turned the pages to *Angelic Ghosts*.

Angelic Ghosts

A basket of apples
One for angelic duty
Not mere samples
To be perfect beauties

I select the roundest

SUMMER'S SWARM

Who needs big shoulders
As I am boundless
Found him under boulders

Sharp as the sword
Their skill must coincide,
When simple rocks poured
They could not hide.

Past, best friends
Though he stumbles
I came to mend
He will not grumble

Will is his need
His body yet strong
Toward powerful enemies
Clever, he must prolong

Protect his child
While he revives
Then side by side
The enemy shall die

Kendrick swallowed hard, his chin in his hands, while he read the dark poem once more. Again his heart was beating strong, but this time motivated by an unknown fear in an unfamiliar setting.

->>><<<-

Since the visions, Kendrick understood why his dedicated father was always tired—he simply never slept. Kendrick attempted to nap when time permitted, but his mind took advantage of the undivided attention. The last thing he remembered was thinking tonight would be abnormal, for he was truly beyond tired.

Kendrick was happy—he dreamt he was floating. From above, he gently moved at will a safe height from the two wolves loping peacefully into the herd of two hundred, without altercation. Their focus was a deer dragging a broken front leg. To clear some of the fawns out of their path the wolves nipped the young deer heels. Fourteen adult and young wolves watched.

Much like the two wolves, Kendrick moved with great precision observing every slight movement, floating, he felt the raw muscular power of the wolves; the subtle maneuvering as they controlled the herd and their prey and the quick culling afforded the pair. When they had accomplished their goal, the rest of the pack moved in for food and the deer herd ran away.

He felt the wisdom of the wolf pack—had they attacked the herd it would have scattered and more deer than they could eat would have died.

He awoke fully refreshed and his mind was clear—two hunters can remove just enough to save the whole herd.

->>><<<-

Lord Randolf's few remaining teeth were dingy dirt yellow. Half his baldhead was covered with long, greasy, unkempt hair that reminded Malus of an army helmet that flared at the top of the neck. He refused to let anyone cut his hair and as a consequence one side was longer. His fingernails and toenails were black.

Today was a year since Malus had started to work for Lord Randolf to gain membership into the army. He had learned the arts of distraction, hide and steal and split running.

Malus's patience with his bare foot leader finally crumbled like three-day-old bread. For Malus, the soon to be scuffle had started that morning when he had halted a plan to steal sea bass. He thought there were an unusual number of people patrolling the dock area and worried they might be waiting for the orphan army. When they returned, Randolf scolded Malus for weak decisions that would lead to the army's hunger this evening. Malus's jaw muscles were rigid. He rolled his eyes when Randolf checked to see who was watching, walking away before Randolf had finished with his tirade.

Occasionally, Randolf stepped on a thorn. Malus thought the 'lord' deserved the painful task of finding thorns as he was always shoeless.

"How many times have I told you to check your shoes for thorns?" Lord Randolf shouted, grabbing one boy's hair, slapping the unlucky lad and taking several short glances at the approaching Malus.

Malus knew the thorns could have dropped from anyone's shoes or pant legs, but that thought never seemed to enter Randolf's weak mind.

"But I did check my shoes," the boy replied.

Malus hoped that steam was not escaping from his ears giving Randolf a clue. The thorn stunt reminded Malus of Ulster—any tiny act that allowed him to control was exaggerated for effect.

Randolf prepared to slap the boy, but Malus was too quick for him. He grabbed the lord's forearm stopping the hand. Randolf attempted to counter punch, jab and kick the boy—all were blocked by Malus.

Lord Randolf wrapped Malus in a bear hug causing him to panic. Lord Randolf's large hands were like Ulster's, but unlike the former head master, Randolf would not be taking him to be whipped or confined. Though Malus was a big boy he was doomed if Lord Randolf, three times heavier, squeezed. Malus could feel Randolf's arms positioning to constrict his breathing. He had only seconds to live.

With the heel of his palms he struck Randolf under the chin with his full strength. The temporary relief was enough for Malus to push against Randolf's shoulders and free himself. He promptly kicked Randolf above the knee. And for self-satisfaction, Malus stomped on Randolf's toes.

Randolf grabbed a shovel from the tool rack. Swinging as hard as he could was not enough to strike Malus who ducked below the flight of the spade. He stood and punched Randolf below the Adam's apple.

He held his throat with one hand and waved Malus off with the other.

Malus waited for Randolf's to clear his head and calm his heartbeat.

"You can leave tomorrow morning. But you best be gone by noon," Malus said.

Very carefully, over the next two weeks, Malus traded extra food with villagers near the four warehouses for cots, blankets, buckets, used clothing and shoes. He promised the villagers the army would not steal from their gardens. He announced a new split for the items returned to the barn—Randolf's twenty-five percent was reduced to ten percent for Malus, sixty percent for the army and the remainder for the boys. Once a week, with an extra helping of food, he awarded the boy with the best escape story, the boy with the most stolen food and the boy with the cleverest new tactic.

The Vlada Boys Army had become a powerful force within the city. A year under Malus's control, there was less city crime, but the taxpaying landlord and merchant complaints had increased.

Two Assassins

The *Lovely Rose* poem and the wolf dream convinced Kendrick a small special team could end the marching hoards. He interviewed Long Bow Knights assigned to the quick-strike teams that had engaged Argo's militia. Kendrick talked with Zachary to understand how Argo's militia had self-dispersed when left without a leader.

Kendrick was a hundred feet from the barracks when through the window he saw Oscar pacing in his quarters.

Closing the captain's door he said. "Have you time to discuss a scheme? If you are pondering another issue, I am happy to wait."

"Son, we have worked together enough I know when you come it is with a serious problem," Oscar replied. He pointed to the made cot.

"Analyzing the options for keeping Madison safe before, during and after the flight on the ancient bird, I have settled on a preferred scheme."

"Did you say *before*?"

"Of late I have presumed if we have visions that the marauders may also have them," Kendrick replied. "I have considered they interpret their visions with a favorable ending for them."

Oscar rubbed his hands across his hair. After a minute, he looked to Kendrick, "Good thinking."

"My conclusion is we need to solve our problem with a tactic so bold that a vision could not *anticipate* or reveal the scheme—pre-empting Madison's need to fly on the ancient bird," Kendrick said.

"So far, I like what I am hearing. What is your plan?"

Kendrick took a deep breath.

"We send a two man team into the frontier with the sole purpose of removing the marauders' leadership. I expect the marauders will disband like Argo's warriors."

"Two men against thousands? Bold and insane enough to surprise everyone—who did you have in mind?" Oscar asked in a confident tone.

"You and I," Kendrick replied. "We will have to live off the land, steal clothing, blend in wherever we are, then disappear like ghosts."

Oscar nodded.

Kendrick continued, "It reduces Madison's risk. It does not contradict any of our visions. And, there are ten years to the next eclipse, if this scheme fails we return with five years to prepare for the battle as envisioned."

Oscar looked out the window.

"How do you propose to find the marauders in the vast frontier?"

"We start by inquiring at ports, trade routes and the clergy," Kendrick replied.

A father's smile favored Oscar's face.

"After we receive the queen's approval, we can go. The Long Bows Knights have a new captain. I like the new Royals Guard Corps and the sergeant has completed critical missions with a graceful flair," Oscar said.

Kendrick nodded. Although the conversation was over he remained seated.

Oscar crossed his arms, leaned against the wall and waited for Kendrick. He appeared to have something troubling him. Oscar knew his role, as a fellow soldier would momentarily be exchanged for his obligation as a father.

Kendrick stood. "You read the poems?"

"Just one poem, *Lovely Rose*. I found it powerful and emboldening."

"Did you find Angelic Ghosts at the other dog ear to be dark and mysterious?" Kendrick asked.

"There were no dog-ears."

"The red covered book was about eight inches by five inches. The poem, *Lovely Rose,* was nine pages from the end and *Angelic Ghosts* was four pages later. The priest said you and Althea had read it."

"Your book description matches, but *Lovely Rose* was on the last page."

Kendrick shook his head. "Strange," he whispered. "Thank you."

"One last thought. You realize if we do not succeed, we will be hunted by a posse," Oscar said.

Kendrick nodded.

->>><<<-

He was dressed as a common man in a dull grey tunic and a brown monk's hat, carrying a sack with food, extra shirts and a knife. He was able to move about with ease at the Vlada port. Though shorter than most, he had no fear in this strange country for he knew how to use a knife.

Gora's six-month journey had produced the same disappointing results. He was preparing to buy passage to port number nine when he saw the crowd gathering.

A large man hiding behind the brim of a black hat was standing in front of what looked like three hundred boys and girls. Thirty armed men stood behind a man in a cloak and a priest holding a Bible.

In a strange way, Gora sensed this was exactly what he had been searching for. He maneuvered through the dockworkers and sailors until he could hear the conversation.

"...cannot possibly let you control the docks. The merchants and warehouses are preparing to oust me from the mayor's office. The citizens love you, but most of the taxes are paid by the merchants."

"Vlada has chosen to close its orphanage. I have taken these forgotten children under my protection and provided them with food, a cot and safety. It seems unfair to burden only the merchants. The dock is a good place to start collecting more taxes," the large man said to the ground.

"Do not force us to jail these children," the priest said.

The brim of the black hat lifted slowly revealing a scarred misshapen face. Gora's head jerked back slightly.

The large man's eyes did not blink and his clinched jaw emphasized the scars. His disfigured hands pointed to the priest. "Why did you close the orphanage?"

"Unable to feed and shelter the growing demand," replied the priest.

"Mayor, I am offering you a solution that is fair to everyone," the large man said.

Gora heard the confidence in the voice. The large man's feet were shoulder width; his arms crossed, he held his head high boldly showing his face.

"Malus, you must leave. If you find a larger city you can disappear into its many streets. We will help you move."

Malus turned to the Vlada Children's Army. "What say you? Move? Or stay?"

"Move!"

Malus turned to the mayor. "We will leave in two weeks when the threat of snow has gone. But, you must provide us with a map to a larger city along with a week's food and water."

"Agreed." The mayor extended his hand. Gora saw the tiniest movement as if the mayor wished to withdraw.

Gora stepped aside as the mayor and priest walked past him.

"It has taken eight meetings, but the outcome is good. I was worried we might have to jail Malus," the mayor whispered. "Ridding Vlada of Malus and the orphans will please the monarch."

"We will become enemies of the city we send them to," the priest said.

"The monarch has plans to eliminate them."

Part Two

Variations

Kendrick felt it in his heart—a sense they had chosen the correct scheme. They would alter the course of the marauding hordes and save Madison from drowning in the moat after a flight atop a large bird. The single black ribbon drifting about no longer made Kendrick tense, for danger was part of the arrangement that he accepted with his life's choices.

The silence between he and his father felt awkward. Oscar had not spoken a word since leaving the castle hours ago. He had grumbled an agreement to Kendrick's comment about the weather.

With only the clothes they wore and their weapons, they crested the road above the port.

"I have a history with the harbormaster and expect he will be happy to make our meeting as productive and brief as he can," Kendrick said.

"While you are threatening the harbormaster, I will talk with the dock worker and ship owners or captains. Hopefully, we will get lucky."

When they reached the dock area Oscar tied his horse to a pole and began to question dockworkers. Kendrick surveyed the dock area before riding up to the harbormaster's house. A tingling sensation shot up his spine as thoughts temporarily drifted to finding Cromwell and Argo on that day he first met this irritating man.

Kendrick quietly opened then gently closed the door.

"What is it you want this time?" the harbormaster asked without turning toward Kendrick.

I want you to be grateful that I have not terminated your harbormaster position. Kendrick wondered why this man brought out the worst in him. "What have you heard from ships' crews or owners about a large army of marauders in the frontier?" He walked to the work area, attempting to stare into the harbormaster's weak eyes while leaning on the desk's edge, but a stain on Kendrick's shirt received the harbormaster's concentration.

"Twice, months ago, I heard crewmembers talking about a bear-like man leading a large body of raiders. But I cannot put much faith into rumors from such untrustworthy sorts."

"Why is that?" Kendrick asked, his heart pounding.

The harbormaster's eyes opened wide as his head tilted slightly. When their eyes met, he stood with the quickness of a wild animal. His chair was sent flying onto its back.

"Their sailors—they live off the captain's food because they cannot fend for themselves. Unsavory characters that depend on lying and deceit for survival!" he shouted.

Kendrick gripped his knife's handle. He felt like killing the harbormaster. He moved his hand to his belt and took a deep breath. Through the window overlooking the harbor he checked the docks.

"Thank you," he said instead, leaving the man to find Oscar.

The bodyguard was maybe eighteen and his intense hazel eyes were reviewing the adults on the dock. His clothes were tattered, worn and an odd combination of blues. His dark shirt was two sizes too small. The collar was stretched around his large neck. Gora wondered if the bodyguard's next swallow would pop the top button.

"If I may approach the leader I have a secret message for him," Gora asked the bodyguard.

"No."

"It is a matter of life and death for him. Do you want to be making this decision for him?" Gora watched the bodyguard stare at the ground and unfold his arms.

He raised his head and leaned forward focusing on Gora's eyes. "Are you sure of your message?"

"Yes, most certainly," Gora answered with a smile.

"Wait here," the bodyguard said. His muscular back reminded Gora of a bull.

Gora watched the bodyguard waiting for Malus to acknowledge him. After the bodyguard whispered into his ear they looked to Gora. Malus waved him to approach.

"What is it you wish for me to know?" Malus asked.

"I heard the mayor tell the priest that the monarch has plans to eliminate you and the orphans," Gora replied.

Looking at Gora's shoes he whispered to himself, "Can I not trust any adult?" Malus raised his gaze to meet Gora's eyes. "Thank you. I will consider your message."

Gora felt his rekindled master plan was being doused.

"I know of a location where you can live in peace with abundant food. The climate is mild and the land open. I can take you there," Gora said, with the smooth tones of an elixir hawker.

"How do I know this is not some scheme to kill me? And why would you do this for me? We just met."

Malus concentrated on Gora's face.

"I wish to return to my homeland. Like you, I am an orphan. I have great sympathy for your cause to rescue and care for our comrades. Hopefully, my travel experience you will find to be of value." Gora knew this to be part truth, part lie, but Malus's smile revealed he accepted the answer as whole truth and the tension in his disfigured face disappeared.

"Come with me. I would like to discuss your homeland," Malus said.

"Certainly. Lead the way."

Malus turned to leave the dock not catching Gora's wink and smile to the bodyguard.

"Did those scars come from an accident?" Gora asked Malus.

"No. They are from a beating."

"No one deserves that much beating. Especially someone as kind and caring as you." Gora lifted his chin and stared intently into Malus's eyes. He saw a slight smile momentarily distinguish the scarred face.

"What makes you say that?" Malus asked.

"All these orphans under your protection are depending on you, like a father, for shelter and food," Gora replied. Malus removed his hat, brushed his fingers through his long black hair and returned a wide smile to Gora. "Has justice been served on your attacker?"

"No. It is not likely to happen. He is protected by the wilderness far away from the nearest village."

"Then you must balance the scale. If you let the beating go unchallenged your doubts will consume you and make you weak."

"Understood," Malus nodded crisply, holding his hat in one hand while the other stroked his chin. A minute later a pleasant grin ended the silence. "Tell me about your homeland."

"Thousands of acres are planted in vegetables and equaled only by groves of fruit trees. There are wheat and cotton fields in the south. Gentle spring rains water the crops and leave behind a wonderfully mild climate. There is an abundance of domestic and wild animals."

"Is this place far?" Malus interrupted.

In the future you will have the good sense to wait until I finish speaking, Gora thought. He took a deep breath.

"Unfortunately yes—especially with young orphans. It will take six, maybe seven years." Gora heard a deep sigh from Malus and grew concerned. "Your *children* love you and would do anything. You can become the guiding influence they deserve. Think of the satisfaction when they are safe, fed and warm. Malus, you will be a legend and word will spread of your greatness."

Gora gently turned to observe Malus's reaction—the smile had returned. "Will you help me plan the head master's punishment?" he asked.

->>><<<-

"We will have to leave our horses at Saraton," Kendrick said.

"Maybe the blacksmith will remember you. I suggest we sell our horses to him, then use the gold to buy replacements in the frontier," Oscar replied.

Kendrick leaned forward and stroked his horse's neck.

"I hate to sell my horse, but it is the logical decision."

"I understand." A few moments later Oscar asked, "What happens if we ride to the far edge of the frontier and we have missed the marauders?"

Kendrick scratched his temple. "I have wondered that myself and originally thought to cross the frontier in a pattern like a snake slithers. But that method left considerable opportunity to miss the marauders as half the time we could be traveling in the north while they were in the south. But, I have recently considered following the trade routes where we will meet travelers from various regions who might know of a menacing horde. Thousands of marauders cannot easily hide from hundreds of traders crisscrossing the frontier."

Oscar grinned. "Son, a clever scheme using the traders as unwitting spies and allies."

Kendrick's head rose slightly. "Thank you."

A few moments later, Oscar's uncontrollable cough began a minute of hacking, spitting and clearing. Kendrick had not paid much attention to his father's cough until three years ago when the frequency of coughs began to interrupt meetings.

"Did you know Quentin has studied herbs? He gave me these leaves to chew on and they soothe the scratchy throat for a few hours. I saved the last bit of Quentin's leaves for close contact with the horde. For now, I will cover my mouth to muffle the noise," Oscar said. "Else, you might have to do the spying while I wait at a safe distance."

"We will be fine," Kendrick said. *I have probably put my hero in danger and should have left him home for his safety. But I could not imagine this dangerous trip with anyone else.*

After a mile of silence Oscar cleared his throat. "The sergeant and I left the team while we were spying on Worchester to gather food. We found a deer and were preparing to shoot when

I coughed. It was a different cough. I knew then something was wrong. To my surprise, it has been a slow growing problem." He swallowed slowly then cleared his throat again.

Kendrick again wondered if Oscar could read his mind.

"We will be fine," Oscar said.

->>><<<-

Evening's light was subdued under the old growth tree canopy. Fresh campfires were carefully sheltered with cupped hands as the starter gently blew on the smoky moss. Flaps had been darkened when tents were erected too close to the flames.

"This is our *home*," Malus said as he swept his hand. "We have more than tripled in the past two years as more and more street orphans have joined the Vlada Children's Army. Luck has blessed us with a variety of ages, wishes and skills. New members are allowed to pick their neighborhood task and our critical functions are well staffed."

"Excellent. You should be proud of your accomplishments," Gora said. "You will need to focus on preparation for battles as the army encounters bigger villages and cities." *I must alter your perception of leadership. Your training begins soon.*

Malus stopped at a slightly larger tent with a ring of tree trunks around a burning fire pit. "Welcome. This is my shelter, our council ring and you may sleep on the patch of grass there." Malus pointed to the right of his tent. "For now, have a seat by the fire so we can talk about balancing the scales."

This may turn out easier than I thought. "Do you know the headmaster's schedule well enough to know when he will be alone? It must be a place where several items can be used as weapons."

"Yes, he uses the boy's washroom midmorning when we are in class or working the fields."

"Is this place close to a door?"

"Yes, it is the same place he knocked me out."

Perfect!

"Are you prepared to welcome the orphans to the Army?" Gora asked.

"We have always adjusted."

"Okay then, you should make the announcement tonight that you and a small team will be gone for a few days," Gora said. "What is the name of the headmaster?"

"Ulster. George Ulster."

"I think that is the name the priest gave the mayor when asked if someone should be a witness as they eliminated you and the orphans."

Malus's ears turned red, his face pink. His fists slammed the stump he sat on.

Better than perfect.

->>><<<-

Dearest Kendrick,

Do you believe it has already been a year since you left for the Frontier? Yet, at times it feels like a decade.

Rumors of abduction plans for Madison are still quite frequent. My anger grows with each new rumor. Why do hide merchants think a good use for a six-year old boy is calming the herds while the hunters simply slaughter the animals?

Zachery has created special guards to protect Madison.

Roslyn and Madison are best friends. She teases him and he protects her from spiders. The other day he attempted to teach her to stomp the spiders. She can run pretty fast for a three year old.

Occasionally, I stare at them when they sleep—I can see you in their faces.

Be careful.
Love, Althea

She placed the letter in the box with the others.

->>><<<-

Malus and his six most trusted members of the army traveled through the night to Dashad Wilderness.

Once there, he knelt within the tree line surveying the familiar Nazar Cathedral turned orphanage. *I hope my convictions are strong. This moment for Ulster cannot be undone. Gora expects me to complete this assignment on my own—I cannot fail him. He must believe I am capable of leading. Otherwise, we will be at odds.*

Thinking of Ulster churned his stomach. The beatings he had endured because the Head Master was a weak spirited man that chose the temporary satisfaction of a beating over solving the problem, made his anger like a thunderstorm readying itself to strike.

"The orphans are in classes. Ulster uses this time to bath," Malus said.

"Time to begin." He stood and walked with a proud stride.

He had slipped in the door near the boys' washroom. The emergency bell clanged signaling Malus and filled the orphanage with the shouts, screams and squeals of the children running for the exit where three army members herded them to a safe, grassy field. The two overworked women teachers, the handyman and the priest were separated from the children and guarded by two soldiers.

Malus yanked the sheet *wall* from the overhead rope to find Ulster shirtless holding a washrag in one hand. The Headmaster's eyes were large like chicken eggs. He snatched an empty bucket and threw it at Malus who tilted his head and leaned away from the flying bucket. Carrying the large heavy stick on his shoulder, Malus was surprised at how steady and determined he felt.

"Have you come back for revenge?" Ulster asked. He picked up his shirt.

"Yes, and perhaps more."

"You have a stick and I have nothing." His eyes darted between Malus and finding a weapon. "And, what is meant by *perhaps more?*"

"I see more buckets for you to throw." He pointed the stick at the crates. "And, *more* could include the orphans wanting to leave with us."

Ulster threw another bucket. Malus ducked and ran to the end of the bench that held seven more water pails. He then used the wet floor to slide on his back and knock Ulster down. Malus stood holding onto a bench to steady himself then picked up the stick.

Ulster stood, grabbed a bucket and swung it wildly. Malus assumed that was a defensive maneuver as he held onto the pail's rope. The stick flew from his hand like a javelin, passed through the bucket's path and struck Ulster's chest below the throat knocking him backwards. The clack of the bucket striking the stone floor seemed to begin the wild arm flailing that increased with each slippery step until he tripped. Ulster's head struck the column and his eyes glassed over. A couple of blinks later, he was dead.

I feel satisfied, yet horrible. Gora warned me about this moment. He seems to know a lot about different things. Perhaps it is good we met. Malus stared at the ghostly face and thought about the beating Ulster had given him before dumping him in the mud.

He kicked Ulster's dead body, happy for the final release of hate and pain.

Despite traveling on hot sandy or cold icy roads, traders had an appearance—furry hats with earflaps, beards, long fur coats over a couple of shirts, puffy coat pockets usually carrying gloves, double layer pants held up by suspenders and boot-tops covered by pant legs. Kendrick's best guess at the color was *drab*. Traders carried their weapons on the outside of the abundant clothing. Oscar had commented traders looked the same at a distance and up close it was only the skin color, missing teeth, facial scars and eye color that aided in telling them apart.

Two close encounters at the point of a sword had altered the questioning of frontier traders. The precarious merchant life made traders cautious—most had been robbed once and now employed mercenaries.

Kendrick tied the white rag on the tip of his bow as he approached the ten men and five single mule wagons. Trader swords were drawn at first sight. Kendrick moved his hands in

73

front of him as his horse walked slowly on the gravely dirt trail. *I wonder if this will ever be easier?*

"Greetings, I am Kendrick of Manshire authorized by my queen to find a quicker and safer path to the frontier's trading cities."

The wagons stopped when the lead driver held up his hand. Clothed in drab his graying hair and beard melded with the fur hat. Alert, scanning green eyes told Kendrick to be careful as he was probably looking for his other men, perhaps including the three men riding the trail thirty minutes ago.

"I am Arthur of Maloon. I offer our services if your queen would be interested in supporting my skilled tradesmen?"

After three such conversations Kendrick had decided "supporting" was trader talk for 'you will never see us, or your money, again'.

"We have heard rumors of a vast army in this part of the frontier," Kendrick said. He lowered his hands sparking a quick reaction from the traders' swords.

"Whoa," he responded and raised his hands.

Arthur's eyes stopped scanning and were not focused on Kendrick, but something or someone, like Oscar. He slowly turned in the saddle and saw his father and three escorts. "Are there others?" Arthur asked.

"No, sir. Just my father and I."

"You are in dangerous territory. You should have more men."

"That is what we thought passing your three man patrol," Kendrick said.

Arthur smiled then pointed over his left shoulder. "Four days ride we crossed a swath of trampled grass and bushes. Thought it was herds of reindeer until we saw the campfire pits."

"Thank you," Kendrick said.

Oscar stopped next to Kendrick. "Are we done?"

"Yes. Arthur from Maloon has graciously provided us with valuable trade information," Kendrick replied.

Oscar nodded his head toward Arthur. "Thank you."

They rode past the wagons and continued without looking back.

Hundred Year Flood

Each Saturday since Kendrick's departure, Althea had taken the children to the boulder field for lunch and afternoon games. She enjoyed the joyful sounds of Madison and Roslyn playing tag and hide n' seek—being with her children was the only activity that filled Althea with joy.

Occasionally she brought paper and charcoal. Roslyn had an artist's eye. Detail and use of shadows made her drawings of animals, scenery, birds and people elegant. Madison's drawings were more playful as he would make a subject's feature's distorted. Occasionally, he would draw something frightening like birds rising from a fire or a black bear riding a dragon hurling fireballs.

Today's afternoon was perfectly delightful. A few thin clouds blocked the sun's extreme heat. The rainstorm off to the far west appeared to be heading south.

After a game of tag, Madison and Roslyn napped in the shade. Althea leaned against a boulder after checking the guards at both ends of the boulder field. The rock's shape fit her back's contour and the warmth relaxed her aching muscles—smiling, she dozed.

She was a ghost. Only her dark leather quiver and bow stood out from the white hooded coat. Carried on the breeze toward the large man with the black mane, she pushed the hood off her blonde hair, prepared an arrow, drew it to her cheek and then released it. Clearing the bow handle it turned in flight and struck the faceless man, next to her target, in the heart.

Momentarily she was bathed in confusion, the heavy rain pelting her face. The children tugging on her arms brought her back to reality. Rain had soaked the children's clothing, flowed across the field and filled the moat beyond capacity. The dark eerie sky was cloaked with black shadows.

Her stepfather had once told of a flash storm that had nearly drowned the village outside the castle walls. Perhaps here was another.

Althea placed an arm around each child. "Come, we need the protection of the castle." The knights waved her on as they struggled for traction on the wet grass; the sheet of rain flowing through the tall grass was like walking on ice—Althea and the children fell twice before reaching the drawbridge. The thought of advancing up the slippery muddy entrance intensified her chest pain. Althea rolled her eyes and prepared to risk the incline, but her fear was quickly squelched when she saw two Long Bow Knights running across the drawbridge toward them.

The first knight reached the end of the bridge, lost his footing, slid off the wooden bridge and across the mud and into Roslyn and the queen—missing Madison. Althea grasped the edge of a rock, but her mud-covered hand could not stop Roslyn from sliding to the moat's edge.

"Mother. Help me!" screamed the princess. Holding onto a tree root the current thrashed her like a windblown flag.

Althea, covered in mud, wiped her face with her undergarment. With help from the rainwater she washed the mud from her forehead and eyes. She watched the second guard reach under the bridge's edge. On his third attempt he caught Roslyn's sleeve. The guard lifted her halfway out of the moat and prepared to hold her arm, but the dress sleeve ripped from the shoulder. Everyone's attention was focused on the big splash.

Two guards restrained the queen. One said, "Oscar gave us instructions to keep you from risking your life *for any reason.*"

Like his father, eight-year-old Madison took charge of the desperate situation at the critical moment. He pointed at the two Long Bows, "Save the queen. I will tend to my sister." Before Althea could stop him he dove into the turbulent moat, which had transformed from a deep gentle channel into a raging river.

Madison fought to keep his head above water, avoid the branches from upriver and swam toward the bobbing Roslyn whose arms were becoming entangled in her clothing. He lunged forward and held the dress for an instant then released it when the princess's thrashing foot struck him in the chin.

A harsh searing *boom!* preceded the lightning bolt, which felled a branchless dead tree across the river.

The redirected water flowed under the tree. Roslyn disappeared in the fast current. Madison swam as fast as possible.

"Flaming Dragons!" Queen Althea shrieked. Her eyes widened and her palms smothered her jaw as she stared at the last location she had witnessed seeing her children—and now both were gone. The rain hid her tears as two guards held the queen.

Seconds later, Roslyn resurfaced thrashing her arms and legs and spitting water. In the next second Madison appeared swimming hard to catch Roslyn. "Roll over onto your back," he yelled. "And stop kicking your feet." Roslyn turned face up. Madison grabbed her ankle then used her dress to pull himself next to her. Placing his arm around her waist he kicked across the current toward the shoreline at the outside of the man-made curve. The faster water helped Madison keep Roslyn's face out of the water. Exiting the curve he heard, "Prince Madison, grab the bow." He turned to the voice and briefly caught a glimpse of it. In that moment he felt the hardwood of the bow's lower limb.

Madison collided with a large stone, water splashing. "Direct us to the back of this boulder," he said.

The knight pulled, tugged and pushed the bow until Madison was behind the rock.

Madison found stable footing. He released the bow. The water whirled around his body, acting like an anchor. He took a deep breath.

"Extend the bow for Roslyn," Madison said. "Roslyn, you must hold onto this bow until you are safe on shore. Can you do that?"

"Yes."

"I knew you could." He kissed her forehead. "Be strong."

She gripped the bow with both hands as the water raged.

The Long Bow Knight quickly pulled her across the water, then extended it for Madison.

Looking toward Madison her tense shoulders return to their natural position and the color return to Althea's face.

The six Long Bows collected their charges. One carried Roslyn, two held the queen and three formed a human chain across the slick mud to the drawbridge.

Water slapped the bottom of the bridge and volume of upriver debris had partially dammed the bridge's upstream side forcing water across the deck planking.

"Wait here," a Long Bow said as he rushed across the bridge. A minute later he appeared with a rope—one end secured to a horse and the other cinched around Queen Althea carrying Roslyn and Madison. Two knights tended the stallion as it pulled the royal family across the bridge.

Inside the castle walls the knights untied the rope. Queen Althea knelt, hugged her children and thanked God for their safe return. At that instant a loud thunder rumbled the ground compelling everyone to search for the source.

Althea took a deep breath before squinting to the heavens.

"This must be the hundred years' storm my grandfather talked about," a knight offered.

->>><<<-

Althea sat at her vanity as she wrote:

Dearest Kendrick,

I cannot describe how lonely it is here without you. Our children are truly a blessing and I cherish every minute with them, but they cannot replace your strength, thoughtfulness and comfort. In the mornings I miss your gentle kiss and the effort to not wake me. If confession is good for the soul, I must tell you sometimes I pretend to sleep as not to miss that special moment.

Madison, in true Kendrick fashion, took command of a difficult situation, directed the knights and rescued a child. He is truly a reflection of you.

Our daughter is developing into quite a thinker and artist. Her thoughts do not always take a logical path, but her solutions are most clever. Interestingly, she seems to use art as a time to think.

I look for you each morning from our window. One day you will return. God bless you.

With all my love,
Althea

She placed the letter in the box with the others.

Frontier

At first light the abbreviated existence of a million glittering embers drifted aimlessly above the flames tips' from hundreds of campfires. A soft treetop breeze blended the dark white columns with the lifting fog. The morning dew soaked through their clothes as they lay upon a hastily chosen observation point—a cliff nearly a quarter mile from the nearest fire.

After fifty-seven months of relying on an untested search system, talking to hundreds of traders and following useless tips, yesterday they crested a hill to find the colossal wake of destruction left behind by thousands of marching feet; acres of small trees cut down for firewood, tent frames and horse trellises. The remaining stumps reminded Kendrick of the castle pond willows cut for furniture assembly through the winter. Hundreds of animal skeletons, varmint carcasses and edible roots were scattered like salt on fresh meat. Every hide had been removed from the bones and Kendrick assumed they were tanned or stitched for tents, blankets, or clothing. There must have been hoof prints from nearly a hundred goats—for milk as no skeletons lay on the ground.

Oscar and Kendrick traveled along the edge of the wake for five hours before hearing the noise of a village. A militia detail of six angry citizens with freshly sharpened sticks protected the charcoaled remains of their village.

"Who goes there?" asked the shortest citizen.

"Oscar and Kendrick from Manshire," Oscar responded.

"State your purpose," said the bearded citizen.

"We are here to help clean up the mess left by a horde of invaders that we are following," Oscar replied. He cleared his throat and sipped water from the bag.

"What a strange job," said a thin man. Another citizen said, "He is going to help us in exchange for something." The short citizen shook his head while looking at the powdery trail dust.

"Where can we be useful?" Kendrick asked.

"Ride ahead to the town square and ask for Mickael. And strangers, we are grateful for your assistance," said the bearded man as he pointed down the devastated swath.

"Kendrick, we need to gather as much information as possible. And, that might require us to stay another day," Oscar said when they were out of earshot.

"That should not be a problem. Any group that causes this much destruction cannot move too fast," Kendrick replied.

As they entered the town square Kendrick pointed to a wagon where the ghostly remains of a priest lay with rope burns on his neck. A constable, whipped thirteen times by Kendrick's count, gently examined the priest.

Oscar stood in the stirrups and loudly asked, "Where is Mickael? We are here to help."

The constable turned to reveal whip marks on his torso. "I am Mickael."

"How can we help?" Oscar asked.

"Come with me to bury the priest."

When they reached the flat acreage near the top of the burned hill, the constable placed an iron weight on the blackened grass then tied the rope to the horse's bit, lowered the cargo gate and leaned three shovels against the wagon's side. "We can dig his grave here." Mickael drew four lines in the soot.

Kendrick worried he had sounded too anxious to dig, perhaps making Constable Mickael uneasy, but he knew Oscar was the skilled interrogator. Also he worried the digging would aggravate his father's coughing. The dirt was dark—good for planting crops. It was easy and quiet digging without the gravel, cobblestones and tree roots.

"Are you okay? Do you wish us to clean your wounds?" Oscar asked.

"I will be all right," Constable Mickael replied. "Thank you for the offer." The constable flinched when his folded arms rested against his chest, "What is it you want from me?"

"Information about the horde leaders. But first, may I ask how you received those whip marks?"

"The orphanage had fifty seven children and twenty-six complained to the bear-like man. While whipping he said over and over, 'one lash for each orphan complaint.' His claim was I should have intervened to stop the *abuse*," the constable replied.

Kendrick stopped shoveling. "What did the priest do to receive the hanging?" he asked.

"He was the reason for the complaints. They hung him so the tips of his toes touched the ground. It was a slow, agonizing death," Mickael replied. He rubbed the base of his neck a few seconds then shook his head.

Kendrick sensed Mickael was leaving out a few details.

Mickael continued, but he looked away as if talking to himself, "Most were quite well behaved and their common goal was to find a home...and a mother. But you had to keep in mind that they are dangerous children who had burned down several villages."

"Children?" Oscar and Kendrick queried together.

"Yes, children from babies to young adult. And they are surprisingly single-minded toward their goal of a home, respect and a mother."

Kendrick and Oscar passed glances between them. They were surprised again when the constable revealed that in the four days the horde had camped at the village there had been no other citizen deaths.

Back in the town square, several villagers commented on the *attackers'* high desire to find a home.

The following morning thankful villagers wished them well.

Oscar and son rode until campfire smoke warned them their search had become a hunt. Kendrick said it was luck, but Oscar called it a well-designed plan.

When night's shadow covered everything, they rode far around the edge of the horde finding a place to rest. Oscar and Kendrick had warm raw rabbit for supper.

"I hope we do not have many nights like this," Oscar said. He sat on a small grass patch and leaned against a fallen tree.

"That is my thought, too," Kendrick replied while wandering slowly about their temporary station.

"What is on your mind, son?"

Kendrick studied the ground before making eye contact with his father. "Did it surprise you the horde of invaders are children? I now worry that I might have to kill one of them."

Oscar cleared his throat. "I have had that same thought."

"We cannot assassinate the leaders, hopefully adults, then leave the children alone to survive in the frontier."

Oscar smiled. "We cannot make any decisions on the sparse information we possess. Since you are walking about, you can be the guard. Wake me in a few hours."

They arrived thirty minutes before sunrise above the eastern hills and would not move or talk until after sundown; Or, if the horde was beyond the western horizon. For Oscar, there were simply too many curious eyes and ears in the horde to risk attention in their direction.

->>><<<-

The early morning sun revealed the travelling orphanage described by Constable Mickael. Within the vast open plains smaller sub-groups could be discerned—older girls caring for infants and youngsters, boys and girls separated by age and older boys carrying food and water.

A bugle sounded. The children began packing. Within fifteen minutes a second bugle sounded. The children cheered and walked to the west. Goats were the last in line and herded by eight singing boys. A hill blocked the front of the horde.

Kendrick and Oscar stared with wide eyes. Oscar pointed when the leaders passed the edge of the hill, two men followed by ten young men who were barely old enough to shave, riding slowly a hundred yards before the horde. Periodically, two scouts returned to the lead group and replaced a pair of guards.

Kendrick turned to him with wide eyes and clenched teeth. Oscar placed a finger in front of his lips. A man with a black bear's appearance rode a black Clydesdale alongside a small man on a brown horse.

->>><<<-

Althea scanned the stars looking for Draco the Dragon and Pegasus the Winged Horse while thoughts of her youth and Kendrick tickled her mind. She had not been this calm since the visions days before Madison's birth. She hoped Kendrick was watching Pegasus—perhaps they might have a dream together. Her heart beat stronger as a warm sensation filled her with joy.

For a minute she closed her eyes and thought only of her husband in the frontier.

Tomorrow she would feed the children, escort them to the cathedral library for school, then ride her horse to the grand curve. Why they had to meet so far from the castle continued to unsettle her. But, the sergeant insisted it was Kendrick's wish.

->>><<<-

Kendrick searched the stars for Pegasus. The dreams of his youth were jumbled together. He wished the winged horse would take him to Manshire tonight for dinner, a dance and a visit with their children. His heart ached for a moment with Althea—someone to listen to him. In that instant he felt a wave of joy like his first kiss, starting at his heart and quickly filling his entire being.

Wooden Angels

Kendrick released the arrow and it found the pheasant just below the neck. Another night of raw meat; at least tonight's dinner would be more tolerable.

Oscar sat on a log whittling on a thumb-sized branch of soft wood. Kendrick had watched him only once before—the night before leaving to stop the northern marauders. Mother's disability had confined her to bed and the weather was turning bitter cold. Both events had a common ingredient—his duty conflicted with his sense of doing the right thing.

Kendrick cleaned the pheasant and sliced off the meat.

Oscar finished whittling the small wooden angel, gently wrapped it in the rag with the other two and placed it in his pocket. "A little gift to remember this adventure." He replaced the knife in the scabbard. "We have three choices, all of which are bad. We assassinate the leaders and let the horde scatter where they may. Or, we assassinate the leaders and lead the children ourselves. Our last option is to assassinate the leaders before they land on Estmira."

"None of those options are appealing to me," Kendrick replied. "The children will likely attempt an attack on Manshire if they are only a few days from the castle."

"I agree. If they have been deceived they will take their anger out on Manshire. The older boys will feel indestructible. I recommend we continue spying. Another option may present itself."

"Under what conditions would we take out the leaders?" Kendrick asked.

"It would have to be somewhere the children could be housed rapidly. Maybe near a large city, or several close villages."

->>><<<-

His shoulder was shaking and his father was in his head, "Wake-up. We have spying to keep us busy today." Kendrick had always respected his father, but this journey had opened his mind to the whole man. In spite of the hardship that naturally accompanied this mission type, as well as his ailing health, each morning Oscar presented his best smile—he was not *all* business. His job had not jaded him...completely.

We have a good relationship in spite of the risky nature of our jobs; but, maybe it is precisely that understanding that any mission might be the last, which makes us appreciate our time together.

"Come, Kendrick, we have to see what the children are up to today. I gathered some roots while you were hunting last night. We should consider camping farther out, cooked meat would be nice."

Kendrick's fingers combed his unkempt hair. "Okay, I vote for a fire tonight." A deep breath made him cough. "What is that awful odor?"

"I think they are aurochs, the last wild cattle herds. They arrived here ten minutes ago. A rather rude awakening," Oscar said.

A loud snort startled them.

Kendrick leaned forward, rubbed his eyes, then looked into the dark aurora. A reflection of the moon in hundreds of large eyes was like floating in an ocean of stars. "How did they manage to arrive so quietly?"

"It appears they stroll and chew silently," Oscar said as he mounted his horse.

They moved slowly through the herd.

"I wish Madison was here to see this." Kendrick stared ahead for a minute. "I miss my children."

"It gets harder with each mission," Oscar said. He coughed. "It leaves you with an empty feeling and only your child's hug can satisfy. The hardest departure was a few days before your mother's death. I should have challenged the king for a delay." Kendrick saw the silhouette of Oscar's hand wipe his eye.

Kendrick smiled for he understood his father. He felt the emptiness growing each day.

"You know how I felt when you were growing up," Oscar said.

"Yes...yes." Kendrick whispered, wiping each cheek.

Twenty minutes later, they were hidden under an overhanging cliff and behind a five-foot embankment created from the plate sized stone slabs falling from above. Kendrick worried that this observation point might become a deathtrap at any moment. The stanza from *Angelic Ghosts* repeated in his mind.

Sharp as the sword—Their skill must coincide. Oscar diligently expressed the value of keeping weapons sharp and sparring with other knights. Although he was no longer the captain he emphasized the need to analyze and prepare for conflicts. A *Complete* knight is what Oscar called them if they had superior weapons skills and had developed analytical skills to avoid combat if possible. Kendrick knew of only three complete knights—Oscar, the sergeant and Zachery.

To Kendrick, the nature of spying was time wasted waiting for something to happen or someone to follow. After an hour, Oscar shrugged. Kendrick nodded. A slab fell from the ceiling. Both men flinched.

When simple rocks poured—They could not hide. The clack of the slab on the embankment sent his heart racing. Kendrick hoped something, *anything,* interesting would happen to keep his mind off those large fractures.

Oscar and Kendrick watched as the orphans filled their day repairing trellises, cleaning clothes, bathing, sewing tents and other nomadic needs.

Walking, talking and laughing with the orphans had consumed the day for the large dark haired leader. He ate and drank as he moved about.

By mid-afternoon, Kendrick wanted to risk being caught— the boredom was intolerable.

->>><<<-

Althea cautiously entered the grand curve. She was considering a quick return to the castle, but it was the sergeant that insisted. He had been with her most of her life—a personal guard, partner in revealing the archbishop's scheme, bodyguard and now the head of her clandestine corps.

She dismounted and walked into the forest. After three minutes she looked to the sky. *Where is he?*

A few moments later, she heard a horse galloping toward her. *I should not be here, alone. Manshire needs a queen, prince and princess. Return to care for the children and rule the country is my obligation. This place has been a safe haven, but times have changed.* Althea climbed onto her horse. Tugging the reins to escape from the other entrance she heard a loud whistle.

"Queen Althea. I am late. Please forgive me," the sergeant shouted as he stopped his horse.

"I have been here only a few minutes myself."

"Thank you, my queen. You are so gracious," the sergeant said.

"Why are we here?" she asked.

"Archery lessons. That is why I am late. I forgot the bow Kendrick left for you."

"Archery lessons?"

"Queen Althea I have a letter for you."

"Please open it," the queen said.

The sergeant slipped his knife under the fold and sliced. He handed the letter to the queen.

Althea,

   It has been five and a half years since my departure and hopefully I will see you within the next few years after successfully disbanding the horde.

   The sergeant has my gift to you, a bow. If I do not return you will have this bow to remember me by. But, more importantly, you will be able to protect our children in my absence.

SUMMER'S SWARM

When you can see the flight of the arrow before its release, your training is complete.
Tell the children I love and miss them.

With all my love,
Kendrick

She sighed and used her shirtsleeve to wipe her eyes. "Okay Sergeant. Teach me."

->>><<<-

Kendrick tapped Oscar's shoulder. "Father, it is time to go."

Oscar woke with a barrage of coughing, throat clearing and spitting.

"Father, are you okay?"

"The disease is advancing faster with our poor living conditions. I worry that my cough could expose us. Two of Quentin's herbal leaves seems to work for most of the day, but it requires more over time," Oscar said.

From a distance, the campfire's orange hue reflected off rock formations and trees defining the orphans' camp.

Oscar rode up alongside Kendrick and whispered, "We should find the leaders' camp. A night raid might be the best option."

Kendrick tapped Oscar's sleeve and pointed to the west where the torches' flames were yellow.

They dismounted, tied the reins to a front hoof, carefully hid their metallic weapons, then crawled between the short bushes to a cliff above the leader's camp.

Oscar tapped Kendrick's arm then pointed at the small man wearing a monk's hat.

A nervous shudder rippled through his back and shoulders. Every breath came quicker than the last. He blinked several times, rapidly, then stared at the face below the brown wide brimmed hat—it was Argo, the son of the exiled Saraton king who had kidnapped the queen, tortured Oscar, trained warriors to

89

overthrow Manshire and had planned to assassinate Althea, Oscar and Kendrick.

Kendrick removed an arrow from the quiver—his eyes never left Argo.

The soft touch of his father's hand resting on his arm broke his concentration. Oscar's arthritic index finger tapped his temple.

"We have the children to consider. Argo and his *black bear* have a firm grasp on caring for the children," Oscar replied.

Kendrick rolled his eyes, replaced the arrow and hung his head. A minute later Oscar's thumb pointed over his back. Kendrick crawled backwards away from the cliff's edge. Oscar followed.

"We let them continue on their journey and complete our mission in Manshire?" Kendrick asked.

"Unless a better plan reveals itself. Did you count the people in the leader's camp?" Oscar asked.

Two leaders, five pairs of scouts and four other soldiers—two plus ten plus four equals sixteen. "Sixteen, but there seems to be more than sixteen—there are empty tents," Kendrick replied.

"That's my point. The extras in the lead group's camp are likely out of sight during the day and apparently some also at night. Perhaps they are a covert protection squad, which might be on guard duty," Oscar whispered.

Oscar pointed to a darker cave entrance. "That should be a good place to watch from. This mission has no easy answers, therefore we must consider every option."

So far, the cave proved to be the best observation location—they could move about and be covered by the shadows.

"What are your thoughts concerning killing the leaders during the night? Let your answer assume the children are cared for."

"A bit of a problem if there were more than twenty men. Hoping half of the soldiers slept through the ordeal might be wishing for too much," Kendrick said.

The bugle sounded, startling them.

"The masses are preparing to move," Kendrick said.

They watched as campfires were extinguished, small children and the sick were lashed to the trellises, tents folded, food stored and all else loaded on the backs of mules and horses. Armed with knives and spears, the boys about fourteen to seventeen years old scattered along the edges to provide protection. The second bugle blared and the orphans continued on their trek.

Whispering, Oscar said, "At this speed they can only make three or four miles a day, with their arrival in Manshire at about three years."

A cloud of dust engulfed the horde.

->>><<<-

Madison had been ill for five days. Althea thought it was lung fever because the symptoms were runny nose, fever, body aches, high temperature and he was unable to keep food down. Bernyce took Roslyn to another room to keep her well.

The smell of food on Althea's breath made Madison spit up the meager contents of his stomach. She rocked him gently while walking about her chambers.

->>><<<-

Bernyce opened the door quietly, extended her head into the room and watched the queen's head fall to her chest then jerk as she struggled to stay awake. Quietly Bernyce closed the door. She turned and bumped into Samantha.

"Sorry," Bernyce said as she started to bow.

Samantha placed her hand on Bernyce's shoulder.

"I have not seen Althea for two days and thought I would offer my help after I found out she was sick," Samantha said.

"Please come with me. You can care for Roslyn while I tend to Queen Althea and Prince Madison?" Bernyce asked.

"Thankful that I can help," she said. "Go, Roslyn and I are going to play hide n' seek."

Returning to the queen's chambers she washed Althea to cool her body, then escorted her to bed. Within minutes she was asleep. Bernyce retrieved fresh water then bathed Madison before placing him in bed. The queen's ashen color concerned Bernyce. She moved a chair to watch both patients.

Queen Althea lay still for half an hour then small jerking movements accompanied the occasional mumbling. Bernyce checked the queen's forehead—normal.

A few seconds before dozing she watched the queen hold up her left arm and shoot imaginary arrows with her right. Althea remained still for twenty minutes.

Suddenly Althea was shuddering under the bedding. A frequent groan came from her throat. The queen pressed her hands over her heart. Just as quickly, she stopped moving. Althea had turned cold and white.

Was the queen dead?

->>><<<-

The small red target had been mystically replaced with a live black bear. She quietly drew the arrow back, then aimed where she thought the bear's heart would be. A loud and painful growl shook the dead needles from the trees frightening Althea. She shot arrow after arrow with part finding the bear. The arrows did not stop the angry black animal from charging. The queen snatched the basket holding the baby and ran.

The bear was gaining ground quickly. Althea's internal debate could not be concluded without action. She laid the basket down and ran away from it. The bear followed her. Her plan had worked. Now the 'easy' part—attack the bear. Arrows would be pulled from the furry black body and then stabbed into the bear's chest. She ran at the bear admiring the bear's long hair moving in concert with each stride. At the last minute she ducked...

Althea sat up. Her nightgown was damp from sweat.

Bernyce watched the queen moving her arms in large arcs and leaning forward appearing to focus on invisible objects. Between each activity she glanced around the room for a few moments. Bernyce touched Althea's forehead, in that instant she awoke—both hands pressing the ribs above the heart.

"My queen, you need to rest." Bernyce held Althea's hand. "I will fetch some fresh water."

The queen sat up, paced, sat at the mirror, examined her weary face, fidgeted with her fingers and requested food.

Bernyce checked the queen before opening the door. "I will return shortly, your grace."

Ten minutes passed before Bernyce knocked.

"Come in," Althea said.

The queen was dressed for travel.

"Prepare to travel with Madison and Roslyn," Queen Althea said as she dashed from the room. "I need to tell the Long Bows..."

"My queen, Madison is sick, do you think it wise to travel with him?" Bernyce asked. The queen did not reply.

The stars commanded the sky and the queen commanded they depart. She and Bernyce, Roslyn, Madison and eight Long Bow Knights travelled north to find Richard's home.

->>><<<-

Kendrick watched Oscar toss the blanket on the horse. After a deep breath he placed the saddle on the blanket. Reaching under the belly he laced the synch strap through the buckle. Satisfied the saddle was secure, he led the horse out of the cave.

Oscar paused, closed his eyes and turned his face to the moon. Kendrick walked by him without a word.

Oscar seemed at peace. Swaying gently with a slight grin, his eyes were closed, his impression one of sadness.

"Think you can find another cave for tonight?" Kendrick teased while mounting his horse.

"I will try. It was the nicest camp since leaving Manshire," Oscar replied.

A moment after resting in the saddle, Oscar coughed then looked at the back of his son's head.

"Bless you," Kendrick said. His neck twitched. The shoulder squeeze had done nothing to alleviate the knot and the uneasy sense that today would have significance.

Although his knowledge of ribbon reading was quite limited, he knew what white and black meant. And, he had developed a habit of searching for them. *I wonder if the ribbons are there and I simply cannot see them in the darkness.* He placed a hand on the back of the saddle and checked for ribbons as far as his sore neck would rotate.

An hour before sunrise they arrived at the edge of a valley. Three hundred huts, four stone buildings, a river and three hundred plus hedged farm fields met the other horizon.

"Now what do we do? If we tell the village, the horde will know they are being watched," Kendrick asked.

"If we do not inform the village, people might die," Oscar added. "The orphans are well organized for children. We should expect some consistency in their operation. I suggest hiding in the square, if possible."

"Not having an escape route, or possibility of escape, concerns me," Kendrick said.

Oscar placed a hand on his chest. "Oh...I am suggesting that only one hide in the square." He pointed at his son. "The other would parallel the leaders. We discuss our findings tonight—hopefully with enough information to conclude our mission. It is high risk."

Kendrick was thinking about yesterday's boredom, Oscar's progressing sickness and how weary they were.

"Son," Oscar said. "I need the rest. You are expert at moving about unseen. I have leaves from Quentin to control the cough."

Oscar knew his son recognized the value and the risk—Kendrick would honor his request.

"Father please be careful."

"The information will be of great value." Oscar removed three leaves from the envelope. "See you tonight about a mile past the goats."

Kendrick nodded and tugged on the reins back-tracking toward the horde's leaders. while Oscar looked for a barn to hide his horse.

Angry Dogs

"Quickly. Take the wagon down the road." He pointed between the two-foot rock pyramids at the edge of the cliff. "Six guards with us to the doorway. Hurry!" Richard said. He pointed at a lone rock outcropping extending six feet above the flat hard ground.

"What is wrong?" Althea asked.

"A pack of wild dogs has inhabited the area. I nearly lost a leg the first time they surprised me."

Althea pressed her lips together and rolled her eyes. She caught Bernyce looking away.

"Why are you standing so far from your door?" Althea asked.

"A vision last night predicted your arrival. Also, the dogs will be here at any moment. *Please* we must hurry," Richard pleaded.

Althea held Madison's hand and Bernyce carried Roslyn as they ran toward the door.

A Long Bow ran ahead to the opening. Four knights encircled the royal family. One went to inform the guards with the wagon.

A hundred yards from the door they heard the barking. A few seconds later and seventy yards from the door, fifteen dogs were growling, drooling and crouching for attack.

The Long Bows knelt and prepared for the dogs' charge. Ten seconds felt like a lifetime and just as Althea asked, "Why are we not shooting?" A pack of ten dogs crossed their retreat. The queen was unaware she had released Madison's hand.

When she returned her gaze to the door she saw Madison halfway to the large pack. His arms stretched wide revealed his whitish skin. Four dogs had bowed their heads, six were whimpering and five remained prepared to attack.

A guard stood.

Time appeared to halt as Althea appraised the danger. *If the Long Bows threaten the dogs, Madison will be the first casualty. If the horse incident was a one-time event, Madison is still the first one to die. He is so calm. The dogs are focused on him. This may be his only option. The dogs appear to be quieting.*

Before the guard could step Althea said, "Wait! He will be okay." Her knuckles had faded from pink to white. *I do not know which is worse, gambling with his life at this time, or the ever present thought he will probably die on his fourteenth birthday.*

"How do you know?" Richard asked.

"A mother knows," Althea replied, focusing on her son, her hands positioned for praying.

With each step Madison said, "Calm. Peace. Rest."

When Madison was ten feet from the dogs, the two who were growling jumped to the left and ran away. The other thirteen were down on their stomachs with wagging tails.

The dogs at their back were gone.

Althea ran to Madison. He was laughing and pushing the playful dogs licking his face. She lifted him for a hug while the dogs jumped up on her sides. Althea kissed his cheek and Madison touched her smile. When she placed Madison on his feet, he stretched out his hand and the dogs sat.

Everyone stood wide eyed and looked to each other for reassurance, except Bernyce.

"Amazing," whispered Richard to himself.

"Indeed," a knight replied.

The Town Square

First light had passed fifteen minutes ago. Kendrick was quickly losing time finding a place to leave his horse and running back to monitor the horde's *personality* as it reached the village. He found a small meadow encircled by willow bushes. The masses slow speed would place them at the edge of the village in a couple hours.

Kendrick stopped to rest behind a berry bush, knelt on one knee and scanned the area. *There! Did that bush move? Was it wind, an animal, or someone's disguise?* He slowly shifted his head. *Another one.* Kendrick had discovered a protection force of disguised older boys, perhaps young men protecting the leaders' flank.

Their natural covering was made of branches from local bushes and attached to the back of a coat. Short lengths of grass, straw and branches covered the coat's front. Longer lengths of wide bladed grass were sewn on the pant legs. The weapons consisted of five short, hand-carried spears and a long knife sheathed on a belt. Their heads were covered with a hood made of long green and brown grass.

As the two rows of four warriors snaked by he noticed the last warrior was about his height and build. Perhaps firsthand experience was more valuable than spying.

He moved cautiously, scanning in every direction before crawling to the next stop. Kendrick had taken forty-five minutes to arrive behind the last disguised warrior and concluded he had no other choice but to strangle him. The orphans were half a mile behind. The leaders were two hundred yards ahead and the closest warrior was fifteen yards in front of him.

Quickly he exchanged clothes with the dead warrior. Kendrick's heart was pumping rapidly. He laid his clothes next to the body, moved the body on the clothes, placed his weapons on top, then tied the coat's arms and the pant legs together. Kendrick had to hide the warrior and take his position before a disguised warrior noticed.

With the body stuffed under a shallow rock ledge, he covered the front with cut branches and four rocks.

Kendrick gathered the warrior's weapons.

Fifteen minutes was a long time. Had another disguised guard noticed his absence? He would never know until it was too late.

Still, he was alone with thousands of battle ready orphans with nothing to lose. Ten minutes of wondering if he would see Oscar tonight kept his mind busy until the bugle blared. The rumble of the horde went silent. Kendrick watched the other disguised warriors running toward the leaders.

Sweat began to collect on the sleeves and torso of the disguise warning Kendrick of the rash that would follow for a few days.

The man on the black Clydesdale raised his hand and the warriors stood in place. Kendrick's quick estimate was twenty-five warriors. He could feel the blood rush from his head as a third of the warriors discarded the disguise and another ten removed their coats.

Approaching from the west were twenty armed men wearing metal chest plates and open-faced armor helmets, their swords drawn merely for show.

"You must be Malus, the Leader," the grey haired knight said to the big man riding the black horse.

"Yes. What brings you to us?" Gora asked.

Malus turned slowly and stared into Gora's eyes.

"We seek to camp outside your village for two days as we replenish our supplies and rest from a long journey," Malus said, speaking to the grey haired knight while looking at Gora.

I wonder how Argo got involved in this. They are having control problems. Oscar will find that amusing.

"Rumors claim you have destroyed several villages," Greyhair responded.

"Because they lied to us." Malus raised his hat brim and exposed his scars to the village detail.

"That is unfortunate. Would you like us to pray for you?"

Malus was prepared to speak, but Gora interrupted, "That will not be necessary."

Malus's face flushed red. "We need to speak with any orphans, the head master and the constable." He held out his hand stopping Gora.

Argo and Malus—neither is happy with the other. This could be significant?

"We anticipated your request based on stories from traders passing through. By law, we have placed all the orphans in homes—total of seventeen. The head master and constable are hunting. You are invited to use the area outside the city, but we recommend water from the wells along the village streets," Greyhair said.

Malus forced a smile. "You are most gracious. Please be patient with us as we are mostly children. Should we cause any problems for your village, please see me."

The militia bowed and returned to the village.

Malus pointed at his bodyguard Vee, who rushed to his side. "I think he is lying, find the truth."

"Yes sir. Consider it done."

"Gora would you like to visit the town square?" Malus asked.

"Sure," Gora offered a nervous reply.

Argo is going by Gora, interesting. Soon someone will have to decide which name to put on his grave marker.

Malus placed his hand on his chest and swiped it to the right. The disguised warriors disappeared into the forest.

Kendrick's heartbeat slowed to normal. He scurried away toward the dead warrior. *Hopefully, the horde's advanced position will not prevent me from gathering my weapons.*

->>><<<-

"I was impressed with Madison's gift," Richard said.

"It has become the subject of several conversations. I hope we can keep yesterday's event a secret." Althea glanced momentarily at Madison then back to Richard.

"You came to talk about your dream?"

"Yes. A black bear attacked when I was alone with baby Madison."

"Was the baby in a basket?" Richard asked.

"Yes."

"Are you sure it was Madison in the basket?" Richard asked.

Althea placed her palms on her cheeks. Her hands slowly slid down her face while she stared at the floor between them. "I remember it as Madison."

"Please continue."

"I attempted to kill the bear but my arrows just stuck in his fur. Picking up the baby basket and running, I felt the bear was chasing me. It was a difficult decision, but I placed the basket on the ground and turned right. The bear followed me," Althea said.

"Were you planning to challenge the bear in *hand-to-hand* combat?" Richard asked.

"Yes."

"Your arrows missed the bear's heart, because it is located lower in the body than you expect." He pointed to the area just above the stomach and centered between the ribs. "The dream is a warning. When you are facing the large man with the wild black hair be aware that he may not be the one chasing you, nor the *heart* of your problem."

More confusing riddles and prophesies. Please stop. She rubbed her temples. Her pale complexion, travel weary joints, sore neck and slumped shoulders revealed her exhaustion.

"There are times when I wished we were farmers—tilling the soil, harvesting a good crop, raising a family and no affairs of state," Althea said quietly.

"You were chosen before birth," Richard replied.

Althea stared at him. His expression did not change as she focused on his eyes.

"Chosen?"

"Your children will be your legacy," Richard said.

->>><<<-

At sunrise, the village streets were empty. Oscar scanned the square. It was not the perfect place, but spies could never be too selective. He quietly moved between the crypts and headstones working his way to the basement stairway of the timber cathedral.

The cathedral was a work of art—perfectly placed timbers, painted woodcarvings on the door and window jambs and massive ornate entry doors perfectly gapped from top to bottom. A yellow and red celebratory drape hung on the exterior banner hooks.

An hour after sunrise a partially armored detail gathered in the square led by an older grey haired gentleman. The square remained empty giving Oscar time to check the basement. He spent two minutes trying to unlock the door only to discover the lock needed repair. After he entered he understood why the lock was not repaired.

The basement was lit by sunshine coming through four windows on each side. Oscar expected a musty smell, but the area was dry. Wooden crates were stored orderly against the wall. The rest of the open room was empty.

A mouse ran across the floor in the auditorium—upstairs, though the clicking of its feet sounded as if it were under Oscar's feet.

An hour later, the clatter of horse hooves and metallic weapons clanging together filled the town square. Oscar gently stepped toward the door and instantly stopped when the massive entry doors' hinges screeched open. Several men were talking as they entered.

"That went well."

"Do you think this plan will work?"

"Not so loud someone might..." He was interrupted.

101

"Everyone relax. You heard Malus say they wanted just two days. We can retrieve the Head Master and Constable in three or four days without any loss of crops...and orphans."

Oscar could feel the pause and it was obvious the *orphans* were an after-thought. The conversations were clear, as if they were in the basement a few feet away. Oscar guessed ten or more men entered before the doors squeaked closed.

The same man continued to talk. "It is just a couple days. Remember be accommodating, friendly and helpful."

The door chattered. Men walked out. The door slam echoed in the basement.

Oscar waited for three minutes then cautiously returned to the stairwell. Before opening the door he suppressed a cough then placed three leaves in his mouth. He wondered if deer felt this vulnerable standing, chewing on leaves; but this might prove to be the most valuable five minutes of his day.

Surprisingly, the activity in the square had blossomed in the short time he was inside the basement—enough activity and people to consider mingling. He knelt amongst three scrubs and watched as the village began another day. A slight shiver percolated up his back and shuddered his shoulders—something was not right.

A light haired man and a fair skinned woman with a freckled red haired boy walked past him. Oscar winked at the boy. The boy turned his head awkwardly back to the side and stared at him, tripping in the process. The father jerked the boy's arm up preventing his fall.

Across the square, a man slapped an adolescent when he dropped a sack of seeds.

A father, three adolescent boys and a son walked rapidly through the square. The father and son had light curly hair, square jaws and dark eyebrows. The boys had straight black hair.

Five orphans from the horde entered the square carrying empty buckets. Two men offered to help draw the well water. Two minutes later at a different well a pregnant woman with three young boys had to hoist her bucket.

Mid-morning, Oscar casually walked across the square. Three young girls were resting in the shade of an old tree. He sat on a stump nearby.

"Good morning," Oscar said.

The three girls opened their eyes and stared at Oscar without moving their heads.

"Good morning, sir," they replied nearly in unison.

"My name is Oscar. How long have you been traveling?"

"Two years," said the tall girl. "Four years," said the girl with the scar. "Six months," said the last girl. Oscar glanced left then slowly to his right.

"Where are you going?"

"To a place we can call home. It is where we can stop traveling and find plenty of food, farmland, wildlife and freedom from oppression," said the tallest girl.

"Yes! A place where we can get the same respect as other children," added the girl with a cheek scar.

Two boys passed through the square. One had six shocks of wheat on his back and the older boy carried nothing.

"Sounds wonderful," Oscar said. "What is the first thing you will do to celebrate your new home?"

"Find a new mother!" they said in concert.

I was not expecting that answer. "I have passed through many countries and there are none with enough mothers for every orphan."

"That is okay. We can share. Look! We have a drawing of her." Two of the girls handed a drawing of a woman with long flowing hair and a beautiful face.

The tall girl rested on her elbows. "We would be happy if there was only one mother. As long as she wanted us."

The third girl began to sniffle.

"Catherine, stop crying," said the girl with the scar. She turned toward Oscar, "Her mother was mean."

"Nice to meet you." He handed them their drawings and kissed their hands. "Each of you deserves to be a princess. I have a gift for you." He reached in his coat pocket then handed each a whittled angel. Walking away he heard their excitement.

He had also studied this woman from the stairwell and the stump. Men tipped their hats, women nodded and children looked to the ground. Oscar felt the activity in the square had stopped momentarily.

"May I sit?" His arm extended, palm up and pointed to the bench next to her.

"Yes, be my guest," she said.

"You are so kind." Oscar was surprised by the deep, silky voice coming from this petite matriarch.

"It would be wise to avoid any visual greeting gestures, which would betray your anonymity. My name is Zelda. My husband, bless his soul, was the former mayor of Pasqueville."

"Nice meeting you, Zelda. I am Oscar." *It was obvious she was a woman of privilege.* The farmer's wives in the square had stooped backs and shoulders.

"I have been watching you study the square from the stairwell, then the three shrubs and the three orphan girls. You have been cautious waiting to determine the rhythm before entering," Zelda said.

You are bold and confident.

She continued, "You have something to do with the massive march of orphans. But you are not with them...I think you are a spy."

Oscar's expression did not change. He must decide his fate with Zelda—trust or move on. Manshire's most trusted knight took a deep breath. "You are correct. Do I need to leave?"

Zelda's hand covered her chin. She tapped her lips with her index finger. "Not to worry. My time here is short. And the citizens of Pasqueville wish I was presently sharing a plot with my husband."

"I have witnessed some odd behavior that I cannot find a logical answer to."

"Such as?"

"Three dark haired boys walking, as if in a parade, a man slapping a boy for dropping a seed sack, five orphan girls assisted by men in the square and a pregnant women fetching her own water," Oscar said.

"Slavery—the dark haired boys are essentially slaves working for the man with the son, the seeds were dropped by a slave and the water offered to the orphan swarm is poisoned."

Oscar leaned forward on the bench and placed his hands around the edge. "Slaves?" Oscar asked.

Zelda drew in a deep breath. "Four years ago the new mayor, an imbecile, hosted the harvest feast. He had his sons clean up. Two were drunk and threw the hog's carcass in the well and within four months the young men began dying, then the young women."

"The decaying hog poisoned the water?" Oscar asked.

"Or the sauce, or it may have been a diseased pig. The contamination infected the surrounding wells and stopped spreading when the hog was removed," Zelda replied. She turned to look into Oscar's eyes. "Or someone poisoned the well to kill for the mayor's job and a few collateral deaths were acceptable."

"I take it the water is still poisoned?"

"Yes, but much cleaner now."

Oscar scratched his beard. "What does the mayor hope to accomplish?"

"The imbecile hopes to divert attention from the orphans in slavery," Zelda said.

"Why?" He already knew the answer, but to be sure...

"Rumors provided by the traders and monks told there was a difference between a damaged or a burned village as decided by the horde's leader. The destruction and murder was based on how well the local orphans were treated."

Oscar's eyes widened. *Water, dead farmers, harvest, orphans, slaves.* "To replace the dead farmers' labor, the village's orphans were enslaved!"

"Correct. The diluted poisoned water will only make some of them sick. In two days they will move on as planned, getting away from the sickness—leaving the village whole," Zelda replied.

"If you do not mind my asking, why are you so *charitable* with this information?"

"I cannot prove it, but my husband was the first one to die from the poisoned water. The new monk pointed out to me that my husband was outside the age range of the other males by more than twenty years."

The clamber of hooves quickly filled the square interfering with Oscar and Zelda's conversation. A quick glance at the big man on his black Clydesdale and the small man on a brown horse, made Oscar flinch.

"I must go," Oscar said.

"I understand." She smiled.

Malus and Gora dismounted and walked to the constable's office. Malus stopped about halfway, placed his hand on Gora's shoulder and rotated him until they faced each other.

"To be clear, the swarm is under my command. You answer villager's questions and contribute information at my will. Quite honestly, if I knew where we were going, we would have parted months ago. I will take my chances on finding our home, if I decide to part from you. And, just to be certain, if you interrupt me in the Constable's office, your last night with us was yesterday."

Oscar smiled as he watched from the stairwell. He was sure Gora was being chastised effectively as his shoulders drooped and his eyes looked away after momentary contact. Abruptly, the large man started walking.

Gora's face was the color of a late summer tomato, as the large man pointed and waited for him to open the door.

Oscar noticed the hint of torch smoke drifted through the air.

A few moments later a loud yell came from the office followed by a moment of quiet blanketing the square. Everyone's attention was focused on the door as it flung open from the weight of the bloody deputy's body.

Oscar's heart was erratically pounding.

"Cleanse this village with the inferno of the abyss!" shouted Malus wiping his bloody hands on the deputy's dry sleeve before slowly extracting his sword from the dead man's heart.

Malus walked toward the cathedral as perhaps twenty young men with swords drawn sprang from behind trees, buildings, fences and rock walls—'cleansing' every man and shouting for mothers with children to leave the square.

Oscar watched Zelda. She had not left the square and sat with her chin held high. He drew an arrow from his quiver preparing to protect her. Her brown eyes found Oscar's and with a slight shaking of her head told Oscar, "No." She was prepared to die. A deep sigh and a confident smile let him know her wish that the evil mayor and his abuse of the orphans she loved would soon come to an end. Zelda closed her eyes as the sword pierced the upper left lung and the heart. Her shirt stained rapidly from the blood while Oscar watched the life drain from her body. No scream—not a sound as her chin gently rested on her chest. He felt like he was watching his beloved mother die, for during their constructive chat he had come to admire her strength of character.

"Flaming Dragons..." Only he heard his muttering as another small group of adolescent warriors set fire to the constable's station, vandalized town square offices and buildings and burned the trees and bushes.

Dragons & Stone

Kendrick watched from a hill as sections of the town were set afire—and thought about the destruction of Manshire if he and Oscar did not find a solution. He was preparing to leave when he heard Oscar's cough.

"Father, what is happening?"

"The deputy was stabbed by the large man..."

Kendrick interrupted, "His name is Malus."

"The door to the constable's office flew open. Malus shouted, "Cleanse this village with the inferno of the abyss!" Young soldiers ran into the square. With swords outstretched, they began stabbing people, burning buildings and cleared the square."

"We need to ride fast. Look at those torches heading right for us," Kendrick said.

"We cannot underestimate Malus. Who uses words like 'cleanse the village' and 'inferno of the abyss'?"

"Father?"

"Yes, we can ride."

->>><<<-

A chilly drizzle developed into a steady rain exacerbating Oscar's cough. The past week of soaking dew, cold raw meat, nippy nights and lack of sleep had exhausted his energy and taxed his patience. He wanted to rest—*now*.

Kendrick watched for any reaction from the horde. Across a black void along the edge of the swarm more torches moved toward them.

Riding hard for half an hour they stopped to hide behind an avalanche in a narrow canyon. Ten minutes had passed without evidence of being followed.

"Kendrick, I need some rest and suggest we stay here. I need cooked food by a campfire and rest tomorrow. They cannot outrun us," Oscar said.

Kendrick smiled. "I could use some rest too," he replied. "I will hunt. Can you gather firewood?"

"Sure."

Kendrick left his horse with Oscar. After five minutes, he gazed in the direction of the horde. A torch's flicker, a tail of a shooting star, or a hallucination disappeared behind the horizon.

After skinning the rabbit he slid the knife into its scabbard. He looked to his left, then to his right. Was the horde in front of him? Or behind? He gazed to the sky—the cloud cover had suffocated the moon and stars. He scanned slowly hoping the blackness would give away a faint orange hue illuminating steep walls of a narrow canyon.

Fifteen minutes later he walked past the avalanche's edge. Oscar sat on the ground with his back against a boulder, his chin resting on his chest. The rare snoring revealed his weariness.

He pushed the stick through the rabbit and poked his palm. "Flaming dragons."

"Warm meat will be a real treat." Oscar yawned, his eyes opening suddenly. "Let me tell you about my most strange day. He talked about the wooden cathedral, the cathedral conversation of the returning *warriors*, walking through the square, Malus, Argo, orphan slaves, poisoned water, Zelda and not protecting her. Perhaps the strangest was a conversation with three orphan girls. They showed me a sketch of the Mother of Orphans they carry in a leather wallet—it looked like Althea. These orphan runaways want a family, respect and love."

"The young soldiers were fast, fearless and deadly." Oscar's face lost all form of expression. "There is no other reason for Argo to be with the horde than to complete his goal to destroy Manshire."

When he finished his story, thirty minutes had passed. Kendrick knew what Oscar had left unsaid—if Argo had been stopped on that ship, there would not be a horde problem.

"My day was exciting, but my interesting single fact is Argo calling himself Gora," Kendrick said.

He approached the fire to check the rabbit.

"How did you get close enough to gather that fact?"

Kendrick lifted his shirt.

"They had disguises? And you *borrowed* one?" Oscar asked.

"Yes."

A couple of small gravel stones trickled down the rockslide behind Oscar.

"Have you thought about how we can stop the horde?" Kendrick asked. He cut a slice of meat and handed it to Oscar.

"We have a large challenge ahead of us for our scheme must be unique and accurately aimed at the horde's weaknesses." Oscar bit off a portion of the warm rabbit. "This is such a delight."

A faint snapping noise came from above Kendrick. He glanced at Oscar already gazing overhead.

"Shhh...." After a minute Oscar continued. "Somehow we need to stop the horde without killing them. I am not sure The Long Bows are willing to shoot children."

"I understand. When faced with that dilemma I had to attack from the back," Kendrick said.

"I had no idea that small archery target behind the farmhouse would lead you to this strange life. I had hoped the practice would lead to better meals for you and your mother. She never said so, but I could tell she was against the knife we gave you. She viewed it as another weapon that shortened your life."

Oscar took an unusually long breath and dipped his chin near his chest. "Son, I have always wanted to apologize for my job as it kept us apart. You grew up quickly, cared for your mother, managed the farm, protected Althea as a princess and patrolled the market. I have the deepest respect for you accepting these adult challenges and zealously completing them with exceptional success."

Kendrick saw the fire flicker in the tears welling up at the bottom of Oscar's eyes. "Father, you were a good example to follow. And, Mother was patient with me."

"Look Madison, a cave," said Bernyce.

A Long Bow Knight cleared his throat.

"How about you check it out first, then I can take him in? It is for his education." Bernyce sat on a rock while Madison explored the bugs and colorful pebbles between the large stones.

With a half frown, the knight entered the cave. He returned three minutes later.

"It is safe. There is light coming through some holes. Do not go beyond the light—there are bats. We will guard the entrance."

Bernyce extended her hand to Madison. Ten feet inside the cave, she heard the knight, "You think she likes me?"

The sandy soil was loose and Madison walked with 'giant' steps. Light entered the cave from holes in the ceiling—some small and others the size of a wagon axle.

"Madison, wait a minute. Our eyes need to adjust."

"Bernyce, what is that smell?"

"I thinks it is bats. When you hear the high pitched squeal or feel the splash of air from their wings, slowly lean over and wrap your arms around your head," Bernyce replied. "If one flies, they all fly. You need to be patient."

"See the slow dripping water from the cone extending below the roof and the cone rising from the floor." Bernyce pointed.

"They will eventually grow together?" Madison asked.

"Yes, but it takes a long time."

"Is everything okay?" one of the guards shouted near the opening.

Unexpectedly, high-pitched bat chirps filled the cave along with the eerie song of a thousand wings. Madison knelt and covered his head. Bernyce moved to his side. "Wait for me before you stand up."

Madison shifted from side to side.

"You need to be still to avoid the bats," Bernyce said.

"Something is poking my knees." He continued to shift for a minute.

"The bats have left. We can stand. Pick up the pointed pieces and we will inspect them in the light ahead."

"This is turning into an adventure. Thank you, Bernyce. Please do not tell Mother."

Light drenched the small skeleton in Madison's hands. "A bat skeleton?"

"I believe that is what we have," Bernyce replied.

The light followed the tiny bones to the sandy floor landing on a strange footprint.

"Bernyce look at these marks in the sand. It is like a large bird's claw."

In that instant, two gold eyes blinked at the back of the room. Bernyce stepped in front of Madison, "Go and bring a couple of Long Bow Knights here," she whispered.

"But, I want to see what it is," Madison said.

"Madison, *please* fetch the knights. I will be safe with this pup."

"You are not afraid. You want to protect it...and me." He scratched his scalp. "Okay, I will return with some knights."

Two knights entered the cave moments later carrying torches.

"Bernyce...Bernyce. Where are you?"

"There. Two-gold eyes," Madison said. The torches lit up the back of the room enough that they could see a two-foot tall trembling dragon pup.

"What should we do?"

"Our ancestors went to a lot of trouble to kill the dragons off." He placed an arrow in his bow.

"Wait!" Madison shouted. He approached the quivering pup with his hand stretched out before him. "Calm. Rest. Peace," he whispered. The dragon waddled closer. Petting the pup, Madison asked, "Do either of you have something to eat?"

"I have some dried, seasoned beef."

"Bring it to me, then go and find Bernyce."

The knights left a torch with Madison then walked further into the cave.

"Stop! The floor turns into a cliff. Look, her footprints walk right off the edge."

"She did not scream—we would have heard it at the entrance."

A knight leaned into the hole and slowly moved the torch looking for evidence of Bernyce's fate.

"This hole is the top of an underground dome. I hear water. Give me a stone." Slowly he counted the seconds until it splashed. "Four seconds, about one hundred twenty five feet."

"Follow me. I have an idea; more accurately, an experiment."

They found Madison petting and feeding the dragon.

"Prince Madison, if Bernyce were here could you sense her?"

"If she were alive and near; but, when you dropped the rock I lost her."

->>><<<-

"I am happy we have a fire tonight," Oscar said, placing a few branches on the fire. "I love you, son." The declaration seemed to come from nowhere as his father gathered his saddle blanket around his shoulders and sat facing the fire. The euphoria spreading through his soul was suddenly choked off when another single pebble bounced off the ground two feet away causing Kendrick and Oscar to look up. Although Kendrick saw only darkness, a chill raced through his bones.

In that moment, stones the size of wagon wheel hubs and potatoes appeared to be raining from the sky. Oscar jumped across the fire and knocked Kendrick to the ground, covering him. Kendrick felt the four stones strike his father's body and the last one hit Oscar's head. Warmth like blood dripped onto Kendrick's face.

The stones stopped.

"Father, thank you for the protection," he began. But his father was heavy, too heavy and not responding. "Please move to the side so we can defend ourselves," Kendrick said hoping Oscar would reply. He pushed his father to the side, stood and looked at the blood stained hair. He gently rolled his father over and found crimson stains on his shirt.

Ribbons of blood and blotches of dirt formed a mask over his ashen face. Oscar was not breathing, twitching, or moaning.

Kendrick stood rapidly as the cold reality gripped his body and the blood rushed from his head—he felt empty. He could not, would not, believe his conclusion.

"Father!" Kendrick's yell answered by the fading echoes—"*father*, father, father." Oscar was gone!

A limb snapped overhead.

He cleared his nose and wiped his eyes before he forced himself to move Oscar's body to the side. He threw dirt on the dwindling fire then squatted to pick-up his father when a small stone struck his shoulder. He leaped fifteen feet from Oscar. Rocks began to rain on the ground between them. He cringed at every thud that struck his father's body. Young voices chanted disturbing weird sounds almost sounding like *death, death, death...*

Kendrick had emptied his quiver at his estimate of the cliff's location. Oscar's quiver was three bow lengths away. The stones were smaller and he had to test his luck.

Placing his right hand as near to Oscar as possible, he reached across with his bow to snag the quiver between the bowstring and the bottom limb.

Three feet away, a rock burst into a hundred pieces peppering them—several sand sized granules entered Kendrick's eye. Half blind and his depth perception impaired, he stretched further for Oscar's quiver as a rock hit on his left hand. The sharp throbbing pain pulsated through his bleeding hand as he cradled it against his chest for a few moments.

He hooked the quiver then jumped to the other side of the narrow canyon. Placing an arrow in the bow, thunder announced the second stanza of rain. Quivering from the pain he drew the arrow, waited and hoped it would only be a few seconds before lightening arced across the sky. For that moment, he could see the children throwing rocks off the cliff. Images of Madison and Roslyn appeared before his arrow. He wept at the thought of killing children and lowered his bow.

The first drops of rain pattered his face a moment before a rock hit his right eye. The ground started to spin, his balance vanished and his trembling legs collapsed. Lightening split a large tree on the cliff. As it fell he knew death would not have to wait long for him as he heard the stones continue to smash against the ground.

Part Three

Alterations

The wind was cold and the sand that rode along with the gusts stung her face.

"Get the wagon ready to return to Manshire," Althea said to one of the four knights. "Thank you, Richard."

"You are leaving now?" Richard asked.

"I have to. Kendrick and Oscar are both in the frontier."

Richard rubbed his chin and looked to the floor. "When did they leave?"

"Sixty-six months and twenty seven days ago," Althea replied. "Is there any significance to the time?"

"I assume they are looking for the horde."

"Yes." She glared at Richard. *Do not give me another non-specific clue.*

"They must be very careful. Their lives are at risk."

"It is Oscar and Kendrick. They are always careful."

"Maybe so. I cannot be sure, but something about 'rocks' is significant," Richard said. He walked away toward the door.

I should not have come here. The conversations with Richard are always direct, but void of complete detail.

She took a deep breath and followed Richard outside. "Find Bernyce and the other guards, we must be going," she said to the knight.

Richard looked to the sky. Althea noticed his momentary frown.

"What is it?"

"The ribbons are confusing me," Richard whispered. "I see one black, one violet and one grey."

"Their meaning?" Althea asked as she wiped her forehead.

"Black is death. Violet is imprisoned. The grey is a life with pain."

"Awful bleak," she said weakly. Althea looked at her pale hands, the spinning ground, the sky, then Richard.

Richard caught her. "She is very weak, help me take her inside."

The knight laid her body on the cot. Richard placed her feet under the elk blanket.

"Please watch her while I make some tea."

The knight nodded without taking his eyes from her.

The next second, she sat up, gasping and holding her chest tightly.

Richard dropped the tea and ran to her side.

"Everything will be okay," he said hugging her.

Tears flowed down her face. "Something is wrong with Oscar and Kendrick."

"I think you are right, but I cannot tell you what the problem is," Richard said, continuing to hold her.

She was calm ten minutes later when a knight entered the underground home. He looked at his queen then appeared to be searching the room for a place to hide.

"Speak."

"My queen, Bernyce cannot be found. We have Madison and the knight escorts. Twice, we have searched the area and were unsuccessful."

->>><<<-

Malus had reviewed their conversation several times in his head. And each time came to the same conclusion—he was unsure of Gora's loyalty and alliance. Yesterday at the village square had increased his concern.

Gora has been taking greater liberties, which chipped away at Malus's authority. Since the burning of Plasqueville, he had had small meetings within the army, without consulting Malus. The bodyguard had attended a few meetings as ordered. His reports to Malus were consistent including the description of The Orphan Mother and preparing for the castle's military resistance. Gora's reasoning was minimizing the unrest he had witnessed in the army.

At Plasqueville, Gora had pointed out the assassin. *He could have not said anything and he would be the leader. Or, what if the assassin was after Gora?*

Malus's stomach grumbled. He scratched his temple. *Why am I so untrusting and frustrated with Gora?*

Doctor / Friend

"Kendrick, be still. I am dressing your wounds."

"Father?" Kendrick whispered softly, "I thought you were dead."

"I am not your father. Be quiet and quit moving. I have to set some broken bones."

Kendrick could not open his eyes.

The next day Kendrick woke and smelled the sweet ointment around his bandaged eye. It was familiar, but he could not place where and when he had been exposed to it. Dressing covered his right eye. Slowly he opened the other eye and moved it gradually through several rotations. A small bedroom with a log and shake roof. Sun entered the room from a small square window near the peak of the ceiling above his feet. Turning his head gently to the side he saw an empty chair, a kitchen hutch with two wooden bowls, strips of cotton and a leather box held closed by a small ivory pin pushed through a leather loop.

"Good afternoon. How are you feeling today? I must caution you to lie still. You have multiple serious injuries."

"*It is you.* What are you doing here?" Kendrick asked.

"I am your doctor for the next few months. The rest you will figure out on your own," answered the old friend.

"What is my condition? I hurt all over."

"One leg is severely bruised, the other is broken in two places, your left collar bone is snapped and one forearm bone might be shattered. Of course there are multiple bruises and your left hand is crushed."

"Is my father alive or did I dream that?" Kendrick asked.

"He did not survive the assault."

Kendrick tilted his head very slowly until he saw Bernard, the hermit that had healed Althea's wrists and ankles, move closer to the bed. He attempted to sit up, but the pain was intolerable. Bernard placed his arms under Kendrick's partially lifted torso. "Relax, let your muscles go limp. I will ease you back onto the pillow."

Bernard wiped the tears from Kendrick's left eye. Kendrick moved his eye from side to side. A verse from Angelic Ghosts rose in his mind, *I came to mend, He will not grumble.*

"We are going to be together for at least six months. You should ask what is on your mind," Bernard said.

"Okay, how is my family?" Kendrick challenged.

Bernard placed his hand gently on Kendrick's arm and a soft smile graced his face.

"Althea is struggling with stomach fever. Madison is Madison—fearless, confident and greets each day calmly. Roslyn is someone special. You will enjoy getting to know her," Bernard replied.

"Will Althea be okay?"

"Most certainly. She would be well had she cared for herself." Bernard wiped Kendrick's face, then checked the splints and bandages. He sat next to Kendrick. "*Any* topic is fair."

"How do you know all of this?" He moved his eye to watch Bernard's face.

"I, as Bernyce, was there a few days ago. But starting today and for several months, I am Bernard and here with you."

"Did you just walk away? Does Althea know?" Kendrick asked.

"Bernyce appeared to have died from a long fall in a cavern," Bernard replied. "Althea knows of Bernyce's passing through Madison."

"Will Madison survive his fourteenth birthday? Who is protecting him now?" The tears had stopped. His eye focused, his face stern as another verse echoed, *Protect his child, While he revives.*

"Oh, I can only talk about the present and past, not the future," Bernard said. He held up his hand. "It is not that I am withholding information, but I simply do not know. But, I can assure you that he is protected."

"Are you an...an angel?"

Bernard rubbed his chin.

"Yes, but for now, I am your doctor," Bernard replied.

"Can you heal me by touch?"

Bernard moved his hand from his wounded friend's arm. "You need rest," He said while pressing his palm gently over Kendrick's heart. "Sleep and get well."

Madison walked out of the cave—the dragon pup waddled three steps behind. He looked to his right.

"Madison, do not move!" Althea yelled.

The pup stepped from behind Madison to his side. The queen and party stopped to study the creature next to the prince.

"A dragon," Richard said. "I was not expecting that."

"I concur," Althea said. "We should move slowly toward Madison."

As the party stepped closer to the dragon, the dragon moved behind Madison. The pup let out a tiny squeak.

"He is hungry and quite shy," Madison said.

"You are not going to feed it, are you?" a Long Bow asked.

She ignored the knight. "Richard do you have food?" Althea asked.

"Dragon food—no," he replied. "But, the cliff ferns are particularly thick."

"He likes bats. There are lots of bat skeletons on the cave floor." Madison reached behind and wrestled the pup to his side.

"My queen, what are you thinking?" Richard asked.

"This is Madison's ancient bird? It will be full grown in two and a half years," Althea said.

"If this is true we have training to do, including testing Madison's and the dragon's compatibility and finding a steady food source." Richard scratched his forearms.

"Are you okay?" Althea asked Richard. She pointed to his arm.

"I am a little nervous. It makes sense to keep it here for a while, but I am not a dragon caretaker."

The only sound was the ocean breeze racing through the wind skewed pines. Althea's eyes appeared to be looking at her feet as she paced, slowly scuffing her shoes on the hard ground. She glanced up at Madison, then Roslyn and finally a pale-faced Richard concentrating on the treetops.

"My queen, perhaps it was Madison you left in the basket," a wide-eyed Richard said.

"Yes, perhaps...but it does not make the decision easier," she replied.

"Wait here." She pointed to Richard and the Long Bows. "Roslyn come with me. Madison bring your pup."

"Queen Althea, we have orders to protect you."

"What could go wrong in the next five minutes in the middle of this windblown wasteland?" the queen asked.

"The dogs could return or the dragon might attack you."

She tilted her head toward Madison. The Long Bow looked at the queen, then the prince. He smiled.

"Yes, my queen. I understand."

Madison placed a hand on the pup's back. Roslyn held Madison's other hand and Mother's. When she thought they were far enough, she sat on a rock. Althea closed her eyes, rubbed her temples gently and took a deep breath of the ocean air.

"My head feels like I am sweeping fog with a broom." She looked into the eyes of each child. "Okay, here is the situation. I am sick and I trust you two to help me make a difficult decision. I need your honest thoughts." She paused, then took another deep breath. "On his fourteenth birthday, Madison is predicted to ride an ancient bird, which I now believe to be this pup. And through this act the enemy retreats, gives-up, or dies. I am relying on you to be your father's voice," Althea said.

"But Mother, I do not know Kendrick," Roslyn replied.

"Then give me your best thoughts."

The silence startled Althea. She expected a lot of banter most of which would be discarded at first.

"Can we wait for Father's information," Madison asked.

"He has been gone for five and a half years. Your father could be dead or imprisoned. He might not return," Althea replied.

"Do the invaders know specifically about Madison?" Roslyn asked.

"My guess is no."

"Can we move the dragon closer to the castle and hide it in a barn?" Madison asked.

"Good thought, but he has to learn to fly. A barn implies people could see it."

"The invaders, do they know any of the predictions? Or, that a dragon is involved?"

"Roslyn where are you going with these questions?"

"The invaders are not coming for Madison. If they wanted only him, it makes sense to do it with a small team. They do not want the dragon, because no one knew about it until today," Roslyn answered.

She can be a clear thinker when it is needed. Madison has never been challenged in a way that requires critical thinking. Perhaps Richard can show him the value. Regardless, if this is the ancient bird, Madison and the pup need to bond. The better they know each other, the better their odds of surviving. Wonder what color those ribbons are?

Althea held Madison's hands as they faced each other, "I would like you to stay with Richard for a time. I will leave four knights to watch over you. I need your promise that you will obey Richard."

"I understand." His eyes rushed to the ground.

Gently, she placed her palm under his chin and lifted. "Madison. You have to grow up quickly, beyond your age. Like your father at an early age becoming responsible for his ailing mother and the family farm. It is in you. I have witnessed it— determination that is uniquely your father's and yours.

Madison reached to hug his mother. He squeezed her neck. She held him, then kissed his cheek. Althea wiped her eyes.

For five days he drifted in and out of consciousness. The only constant was pain, the awful incarceration resulting from immobility and the slight comfort of Bernard's poem *Angelic Ghosts*. Hungry. He was so hungry.

"Kendrick. You awake?" a voice whispered in his ear.

"Yes, a bit." Worried that his voice was airy, he repeated, "Yes, a bit."

"Good. You need to eat and drink some water," Bernard said softly. "Your arms are useless for the time being. I have rigged a lifting device so you will not choke. Hope it works better than my cave table."

Kendrick opened his eye. A rope had been placed over the center roof log, tied around his chest and the other end knotted, it dangled three feet off the floor.

"I have oatmeal with cinnamon apples and milk. Would you like a drink of water before we test my device?" Bernard asked. Kendrick's concern was revealed in his wide eye. Bernard held Kendrick's head while slowly tipping a goblet of water.

"Easy, we cannot have you coughing. I may not be able to put you back together again." Bernard smiled.

"Okay, I am ready."

Bernard pulled the slack out of the rope then pulled to see how Kendrick moved. "Last offer. You ready?"

"Lift."

He tied a loop in the rope and began pulling—two to three inches, rest for several seconds then pulled again. After two minutes Bernard slipped the loop over the edge of the kitchen hutch. He pulled two quilts from under the bed and placed them behind Kendrick's back. He moved the chair next to the bed then retrieved the steaming bowl of oatmeal with chopped cinnamon apples.

"I have milk for later. Take your time. We do not have any appointments or missions." They did not talk until the oatmeal was gone.

"Thank you. The food reminded me of home," Kendrick said. He rubbed his tongue over his teeth to get all the oatmeal before he swallowed "Have I been awake at any time? Or am I hallucinating?"

"Yes, and you were quite lucid," Bernard replied.

"My memories are disjointed and unclear. Did you tell me my father was dead?"

"I am sad to report that he was dead when I found you...a rock hit his head. It would not be hard to convince someone that love saved you. Oscar took most of the early large rocks when he covered you."

Kendrick looked to the ceiling. "What have I done? Bernard, I killed my father!"

"You gave him a proper goodbye and extended his life several months. Had he stayed in Manshire his lungs would have failed earlier."

Kendrick did not care that the tear-soaked head bandages would need to be changed to keep the bad eye from infection. He cried for his father; cried until he could only sleep.

Dearest Kendrick,

I sincerely hope it is that the brightest stars shine during the darkest hours. Without you, being queen has its dark times. Until a few weeks ago, Madison provided a trace of your calming perspective, but he has started living with Richard—a most frustrating, yet kind man.

(I am wondering if Bernyce has somehow become the dragon, as she disappeared at the same moment we found the pup?)

Roslyn has become very moody without Madison— their relationship is much stronger than I realized.

At night I watch the stars and wish Pegasus could swoop down and take me to you, if only for the night. I remember your fascination with stars when we were young. Occasionally, I feel a tingling when I think we might be gazing at Pegasus together.

I hope you are safe and well. Give my love to Oscar.

With all my love,
Althea.

She stored it with the other letters.

->>><<<

As they walked to a small group of orphans waiting by the stream, Gora asked, "Are you that interested in my teachings, or are you Malus's bodyguard turned spy?"

"I am the spy," the bodyguard answered. "Although I have developed an interest in why you are conducting these little meetings."

"The orphans are getting restless. I want them to be prepared for their new home, give them encouragement and let them know that every day we are closer."

The bodyguard stopped. "Is that wise, you could destroy our dreams and visions."

"How so?"

He reached inside his shirt, unfolded a leather cover and carefully lifted a three-inch by four-inch drawing. "Hold out your palm." The bodyguard checked the hand carefully. With deliberate actions he pinched the very corner of the picture, protected it from wind with his free hand, then placed it tenderly on Gora's palm.

He had never seen such a beauty. Hair brushed by the wind revealed a strong long neck supporting a perfectly balanced face. Though a drawing from charcoal sticks, Gora was lured to the confident eyes—he imagined their piercing color. The face was free from blemish, mole, or scar. *I would change my ways to be with her*. He thought back to Lieutenant Cromwell's obsession with Queen Althea. He recalled descriptions of her that were similar to this drawing.

"Where did you get this?" Gora asked.

"We drew them before leaving Vlada," the bodyguard replied. "We wanted to have a unifying and motivating vision of our mother."

A wispy breeze lifted an edge of the drawing. The bodyguard's palms quickly trapped Gora's hand to protect it.

"How do I get one of these?"

"I will get it for you," the bodyguard replied.

"May I use your drawing this afternoon?"

The bodyguard looked Gora in the eye. "Can you promise to keep it safe?"

"Absolutely. You can handle it."

A large smile appeared on the bodyguard's face. He hummed a lullaby as they continued toward the stream. While they walked, Gora plotted how he would use the drawing to his advantage at the meeting.

"On our walk today I discovered the drawing that many of you hold near your heart of the Mother of Orphans. I know of this lady. If you have a drawing, please show it."

A minute later, three quarters of the group held up their drawing.

"Excellent. You can put them away," Gora said. "She is strong, wise and fearless. Protecting orphans is her mission. And yet, strangely, a man much like the bodyguard and a small boy protects her. Her beauty mesmerizes warriors. She uses her skills, efforts and abilities to protect her children—they are no longer called orphans. To be worthy of her love requires each of us to be vigilant in our quest to occupy our future home and insure it will always be for the children."

A cheer caught the attention of nearby orphans. "Tell us again, please."

Gora repeated the Mother of Orphans story.

->>><<<-

"Are you sure?" Queen Althea asked angrily.

"Yes, my queen," the sergeant replied. "I did the interrogation myself."

"Another abduction? And for what purpose?"

"To calm the herds while the hunters kill for the fur. If I may my queen, it would not be an abduction, which returns the victim. Madison would be gone."

"Hides for coats and blankets...Flaming dragons! Will this family ever be free from exploitation?" She coughed while walking toward the window. Her voice was calmer as she turned to face the sergeant. "We just left him with Richard two months ago. Regardless of all this fodder, take your corps and protect him. Send the Long Bow Knights home in case one of the Long Bows is the informant. And, if you have the slightest doubt, bring him home. Thank you."

She was left alone in the empty room; the bodyguards waited in the hall.

Lord, Please guide Oscar and Kendrick on their mission and swiftly return them to us. You know I ask for selfish reasons, but hope my prayer can be answered and your plan still fulfilled. Amen.

->>><<<-

Three months of bed confinement in a room with one window—stars, clouds and an occasional bird, but no ribbons. Bernard's company and diligence made the time tolerable. *He was such a good friend.*

Today my friend wants me to stand, even for a few seconds. Hope we eat first, I feel weak.

"Good morning, Kendrick. It is going to be a great day for you."

"I hope so. Do you think I will ever be able to use my left hand?" He grimaced as he slowly opened and closed his fist.

"Yes, but we can talk about that later. The fact that you cannot shoot a bow is of little importance right now. Patience, all will be cared for at the right time. Do you wish to eat first?"

"You are asking? You already know the answer. Do you think we can talk about Bernard?" Kendrick asked.

"I am open, ask away."

"Are you really an angel?"

"Correct, from a small special order. Only a few angels transfer to earthly bodies. We essentially become human with spiritual gifts and powers. As humans we must take care of the body."

"Why did you take a human form?"

"In a spiritual form, the communication process is planting thoughts, dreams and visions in the calling's mind. It is time

128

consuming and holds less impact. As a man I can have a better impact on the outcome if I choose the right calling."

"You are a good cook." Kendrick scooped another spoon of stew. "How did you and I get connected?"

"I selected your calling over eleven others because I was eager to work with your openness to solving matters without resorting to death as the first option," Bernard replied. "It was determined that your preferred solutions would bring about a shift from 'might is right' to 'resolution by cooperation'. You needed support to have an impact."

Kendrick lowered the bowl of stew and stared out the window.

Bernard watched him for a couple minutes. "What is your concern?"

"Why wouldn't you heal me by spiritual power? Manshire needs me."

"There are others in your circle of family and friends that need to change to support you. And you, being you, would take charge of a task that needs to be performed by someone else. Your heart is in the right place, but it might not be the best option."

Kendrick had a couple spoons of stew.

"Am I interpreting you correctly? I am healing naturally and will likely be impaired to expand someone's capability?" Kendrick asked.

"*Several* individuals are critical to supporting you. Kendrick, I promise you will be whole when this is done."

"Not much I can do until I heal."

"I would like to suggest you have all the knowledge needed to bring an acceptable conclusion to the invading orphan horde. You should think about taking paths that are unfamiliar, perhaps scary for you, or more risky than you are comfortable with."

Kendrick looked through the window. A pink and green ribbon drifted by.

"Healing and peace," Bernard said as he took the empty bowl. "We will try standing after your nap."

->>><<<-

The sergeant and his highly trained team had been deployed two weeks ago around the clearing of chipped rock, wind shortened plant life and dry outcropping, which served as the door. The Long Bow Special Corps had wounded a couple wild dogs to motivate the pack to move elsewhere.

Although the assignment was boring to the corpsmen, it was of major importance. Occasionally, the dragon's antics and Madison's inexperience gave them a laugh, at least in silence. The dragon's favorite trick was to push Madison from behind when he stooped to pick something up.

The sergeant watched Madison and the dragon train together every morning or most evenings. Leather bags of rocks were tied to the dragon's back to simulate Madison's weight. The scariest part of the training was strengthening the pup's roar though Richard insisted a mighty roar at any distance was more fearsome than a few up-close bites.

One morning, following an eventful day with Madison and his dragon, he was surprised to receive a letter from Richard to the queen.

->>><<<-

Richard watched the sergeant at the cave's entrance. Though it was already sealed, he still remembered the words he'd written:

Queen Althea,

The dragon will begin flying in the next two weeks. I do not know how he will react. We could trigger his instincts and become food. Or he might try to incinerate us. Madison is safe as he has a special relationship with him. The pup has grown a half-foot a month and I predict will reach full size in another five months. Madison will be the only one with control of the beast.

Kind Regards

Richard

->>><<<-

The horde had grown by six hundred over the past year. Malus decided no travel this winter. Within the horde he said it was to keep the young from freezing—which was true. But, within his tent he did not want to be caught crying with each death.

After spending twenty days with the bodyguard looking for a safe haven with plentiful wildlife, deadfall, space, wind protection and snow to melt for water; Gora and the bodyguard had become close friends. He'd tried for two days to pronounce Voltinisk Kykyroystic—Gora called him 'Vee'.

"Have you ever thought about being the Lord of the Vlada Children's Army?" Gora asked playfully.

"Only briefly, when I first met Malus," Vee replied.

"You should think about being a leader after we are settled."

"You think so?"

"Most certainly. Malus will need assistance ruling our new home. You have the talent and knowledge needed to be an excellent leader," Gora said. "Let me talk with Malus before we arrive and suggest a battlefield commander position."

"Battlefield commander?"

"You have a natural gift. Malus will be busy planning our attack. When he is done I will discuss your situation with him."

"Thank you."

"You are welcome." *In another five months you will be ready—to kill Malus.*

Moving Oscar

For thirty minutes, the sun had burned into his window. Through the recuperating period waking at first light remained easy, rising from bed was a struggle and putting on clothes near impossible. Kendrick had to start moving; Bernard would be there soon for their first morning walk. He felt a little embarrassed knowing he would be leaning on his small friend.

A few moments later the outer door creaked open. A knock on the room door was sharp and loud. "Kendrick, I have a surprise for you. Are you ready for our walk?"

"I am almost ready," Kendrick said. He had to grasp the side of the bed to keep from falling.

"Kendrick, you should not lie to your angel," His voice almost singing. "I will meet you at the barn. Your gift is leaning here by the door."

I hope it is a wagon and horse for that is the only way I can make it to the barn.

"I heard that," Bernard chuckled.

Then hear this, Thank you!

Ten minutes of dressing seemed like an hour. Generally, his stiff joints ached and his left knee and right shoulder produced sharp pain in certain positions.

He opened the door to find a hand carved walking stick. It had noticeable bends between the five knots, the handle was smoother than saddle leather and it swung perfectly for his height. Below the handle was a carving of Althea, her hair brushed by the wind, a strong neck and pretty face. Though a carving, he was lured to those two blue dots that served as his beloved's beautiful eyes.

Kendrick exited the outer door, his back stooped slightly from the physical wounds yet unhealed. Still, he felt a joy like the birth of a child, or receiving a kiss from Althea.

In a few more days I will be back in the saddle.

"In a few more days you will be in the back of that wagon," Bernard said.

"Thank you for the walking stick. The carving is wonderful."

Two nuns carrying water passed Kendrick and Bernard. "You are making great progress mister Kendrick."

"Thank you." Kendrick turned to Bernard, "I am feeling...ready. Can we leave tomorrow?"

"Not so fast. I suspect you will be very sore tomorrow evening. Which is good. But we have plenty of time. A week's rest will make the long journey tolerable."

"Okay, I trust you." He looked along the horizon and then to Bernard's face, which produced a knowing smile. "I have thought about our discussion, I want to commit to you that I will be diligent at finding peaceful solutions where possible and creating a happy life for those close to me."

"Very nice Kendrick."

A minute later, Bernard's smile disappeared; he removed his hat and looked into Kendrick's eyes. "I thought we might retrieve Oscar's body tomorrow morning, but only if you are ready. Think about it."

Kendrick placed a hand above his misty eyes. Looking at the ground he whispered, "Yes."

Kendrick was waiting on the porch when Bernard arrived with the wagon.

"Good morning. I put some hay in the back to sit on."

"Hello. I am ready." Kendrick found blankets and rope inside the wagon.

Half an hour ride brought them to a narrow canyon with an area the size of a stable cluttered with small to large rocks.

Kendrick could see the blood stains on the rocks. He looked up. *Thirty feet, how could I not have heard the orphans?*

He pointed at an orderly pile of rocks. "Oscar?" he asked.

"Yes," Bernard replied. "We covered him."

Kendrick slowly stepped around the large rocks, stopping by the spot where Oscar had sacrificed his life. He knelt slowly, leaned his walking stick on the grave and prayed silently. A feeling of safety, peace and love enveloped him. His body tingled from the inside out when he asked for forgiveness. Strangely, it felt like flying in a dream.

"...Amen," he opened his eyes. The area was filled with a pure white light.

Kendrick looked to Bernard. His hands held above his bowed head seemed to be the source of the calming light. When Bernard lowered his hands the light stopped.

"I am ready to take Oscar," Kendrick said.

"He is ready in the wagon."

"How?"

"I requested help while you prayed," Bernard said.

At the wagon, Oscar was wrapped in a small quilt gathered in the back. The four panels sewn onto the beige blanket showed three crosses on a hill, Jesus ascending to heaven, Jesus feeding fish and bread to children and light beaming through clouds to the top of a cross. The ropes were cinched between the panels.

The horse whinnied when Kendrick touched the quilt.

Bernard stopped at Kendrick's room and helped him from the wagon. "We can sit on those chairs." He pointed to the porch. When Kendrick was seated, he continued. "Kendrick, I will leave you tomorrow. The wagon will be ready with Oscar, your weapons, blankets and some food and water. There are only two horses in the barn—yours and Oscar's—take them, the nuns do not need horses."

"What is happening?" Kendrick asked.

"I have other work to do. You are safe. We will meet again, but for now, my work with you is complete. Any final questions?"

"Did you have anything to do with the extra pages in my reading of Roslyn's poem?"

"Yes. It was a message from me specifically for you. Oscar or Althea would have had a disagreeable interpretation," Bernard replied.

"It was comforting these past months. Thank you. Good bye my friend."

"Good bye my friend."

->>><<<-

The Vlada Children's Army had survived the winter and Malus had cried only three times. Vee said it was mild compared to the previous seven.

Throughout the winter, Gora found the cold tolerable and visited those he thought had enough character to discuss their frustrations. *Funny how everything is okay until you start to really ask the pertinent questions. Then, the complaints multiply.*

The list of characters was short, perhaps sixty people, but they controlled the course of opinion for the immense camp. Three or four characters in a tent generated an abundance of vocal judgment.

Gora started the tent meeting by talking about a new complaint he had heard—it did not have to be reasonable. His favorite had been "the snow is slicker here." Though completely out of Malus's influence, he was being held responsible for slick snow. The majority of complaints skirted the edge of reasonable—too short of a notice between the two advance horns, no information about where we are, no progress reports and why do the leaders eat separately? *The wine was beginning to age.*

Deflecting attention from himself required a subtle delivery to Malus. "I heard while walking about camp today..." Or, "Let me look into that for you."

From his experience he knew timing was critical. Getting the resentment and lost loyalty to boil when they arrived on Estmira (the island continent of Manshire) was going to take some major planning. Gora had no idea where they were and when they would arrive. He spent afternoons running the scheme through his mind. On the day of the attack he would have Malus killed, take control of the horde and sit back with some wine while all his wishes came true.

->>><<<-

The sixteen-week trip from the nuns to the big oak felt like a hundred. The trip had involved a mountain road that turned upon itself, embarking on an old and tired channel barge, trail finding in grassy spring fields and seeking shelter under the wagon.

Mother's grave faced the sunset and shade covered the site most of the day. This is the place that Kendrick had saved Althea from certain death by four ruffians. An uneasy stomach accompanied any thoughts of going to Manshire castle first. *Must be Bernard choosing to influence me with spiritual hints.*

Kendrick stopped by the family farm for a shovel and an axe. He walked to the back of the house and gathered nine blooming Amherst Roses. Arriving at the big oak he placed the flowers on her grave and talked to Mother. "I apologize for my absence the past five plus years. My plan to assassinate the leaders of the approaching marauder horde has failed. Oscar lost his life supporting the plan." He thought briefly of the joy his parents must be facing now that they were together.

"It turns out that the marauders are orphans—a complication of the highest struggle. I suppose I can tell you, Bernard, the man that helped us rescue Althea, is an angel. But, Father's grave is not going to dig itself. I love and miss you."

He dug for two hours, pulling the horse and wagon near the grave and carefully lifting Oscar out of the wagon. He rested the stiff body in the grave.

"Sorry you did not make it back to Manshire, alive, he began. "Each day the invasion seems more likely. I doubt we have the resources to match thousands of invaders or the will to kill children. I had fun traveling with you, but am deeply saddened by your death...Father, I love and miss you."

Kendrick filled the grave. With the shovel and axe returned to the wagon, he looked at the graves of his beloved parents—perhaps for the last time. Bernard appeared from the side, Abbey and Oscar accompanied him. They appeared to be protected by a halo. Mother's joints looked normal and for the first time in Kendrick's memory, Father and Mother held hands.

A single green ribbon drifted casually amongst the treetops. Recently Bernard had helped Kendrick with his first emerald ribbon that signified his choices brought peace—he smiled.

->>><<<-

Pre-dawn, the Long Bow Special Corps were in place. The last inch of snow had melted and mud had replaced the snow. The mission was the easiest and most important duty they had been assigned since their charter. But the boredom was wearing on the Special Corps.

The Long Bow Corpsmen dispersed to the best defensive positions. Several were stretching their stiff muscles when the thunder of ten horses burst from the tree line. Eight men drew arrows creating a safe corridor for the two advancing toward Madison. The front rider leaned to the horse's side and grabbed Madison. The second rider shot Richard as he attempted to stop the kidnapping.

Suddenly, a whistle came from the woods. Six corpsmen blocked the road and began their attack against the invaders. One, three, four, six had been shot—one fatal.

The first rider had Madison in his grip, a knife pressing against the prince's throat. "Lay down your weapons or the gifted prince dies!" he demanded.

"Place your weapons in the mud!" the sergeant instructed.

Madison jerked when he saw his bearded father walk into the clearing. For an instant the young prince's life was not threatened as the kidnapper attempted to improve his grip of Madison. Two arrows fired from corpsmen found the kidnapper's neck.

->>><<<-

Kendrick limped toward his son, holding his arm as he ran toward him. The embrace was long. Only when a warm tear caressed his cheek did he manage to pull himself away.

"Are you okay, son?"

"It hurts." He clenched his jaw. "Father, what happened to you?" Madison asked.

"I will explain later."

Kendrick knelt in front of his son. "Let me hold you."

A moment later, Madison spoke. "Richard has some interesting books that we need."

A chip off the old block. Business first. I need to change my example.

"We can look at them in a couple hours."

"You okay, Father?"

"Never better." Kendrick continued to hug his son.

The sergeant gestured everyone to stay away, then walked to check Richard.

Kendrick tightened his hug. Madison flinched. Kendrick called a corpsman over to check for a broken bone. The sergeant approached Kendrick. "I thought you were one of the kidnappers with that beard and weathered face, please forgive me. Nice to see you were successful."

"Thanks for your confidence, but success was not ours this time. We are facing a serious threat. How is Richard?"

"He is dead," the sergeant said.

"From a shoulder shot?"

"He lived a peaceful life, maybe the action was too much for an old hermit with poor health. Or maybe the arrow nicked the vein."

Madison, who had walked to Richard's body, stared at him for several minutes, then knelt beside him. He kissed his own hand then placed it on Richard's forehead. Kendrick could see the disappointment in their eyes when Richard did not wake.

"Can we load everything onto the wagon?" Kendrick asked as he looked around.

"And the dragon, sir?"

"A dragon? For what purp..." *Madison, ancient bird, remote location....* He held up his hand. "I know why. Let me think about this."

"Father, do not forget the books," Madison said.

"Come with me, son. Sergeant, please accompany us."

"Kendrick, what should we do with Richard?" the sergeant asked.

"He lived his life here. He should be buried here."

The sergeant pointed to a corpsmen. "Find a suitable place and bury him."

"Yes, sir."

The sergeant walked to join Kendrick and Madison.

"Father, why are you limping?" Madison asked.

"I will tell you the whole story tonight." He pointed to some flat rocks. "Here will do," Kendrick said as he ruffled Madison's hair. "Sergeant, what do you know of this dragon?"

Madison started to speak.

"Shhhh. Let the sergeant answer." He whispered then winked at Madison.

"Nothing, except rumors. Queen Althea ordered us to protect Madison at this location and instructed us to return to the castle if the situation changed."

Kendrick wanted to know the rumors, but decided that the information was not important to the immediate problem.

"I might want to move this dragon. Any ideas, sergeant?"

"Father! Use the books," Madison implored.

"What did you have in mind son?" Kendrick placed a hand on his son's shoulder.

"Put the bookshelves in the wagon. Use ropes to hold them. Cover Phyer and I between the shelves. Carry food on the extra horses."

"Sergeant, I think we have a solution."

"Can you tell me why we would move a dragon?" the sergeant asked.

Phyer nervously shifted from foot to foot while tilting his head and staring at Madison.

"For your knowledge only." Kendrick waited for the sergeant to nod. "We are expecting an invasion and Richard prophesied that Madison, riding a large *ancient bird*, would save Manshire from total ruin."

"This is the first I have heard of an invasion," the sergeant said.

"We kept it a secret hoping that our previous schemes would eliminate the danger," Kendrick replied.

"Where are we moving the dragon to?"

"I thought Three Caves." He leaned toward his son. "Madison, how many books do we have to take?"

"Four."

Kendrick rubbed the back of his neck, "How many total books are there?"

"A thousand."

Kendrick smiled as he looked to the sergeant. "Son, collect the four books and give them to me. Then show me this dragon—Phyer is it?"

"I will begin moving the books and shelves onto the wagon," the sergeant said.

"Think about shelves only in the corners, with enough books to keep them from sliding—then ropes, blankets and rugs covering the open area. And...sergeant place Oscar's weapons on the wagon seat."

"Yes sir," the sergeant said, his voice devoid of emotion. "His death is a great loss for Manshire."

->>><<<-

The wind gusts blew over several tents, but *neighbors* helped reset and stake them. As quick as the storm arrived, it departed. Malus and Gora left their tents to check on the sky.

"Strongest gusts so far," Gora commented.

"I agree. We have endured some difficult weather in this eight year journey. I know I ask too much, but are we getting close?" Malus asked.

"Yes, I do not know how long, but this part of the frontier looks familiar," Gora replied with a lying tongue. "Have you given any thought to your new job when we arrive?"

"Very little actually. Why?" Malus asked.

"Now you are responsible for making decisions for the benefit of the army, but ruling a nation requires different techniques," Gora replied.

"What are you suggesting?"

"For example, the army orphans can steal food from other orphans, because it is for the good of the group. But once they have land and responsibilities to a family, any stolen food likely means the victim's family goes hungry. And you will be the one they look to for resolution. Your judgment must be respected and your word, final," Gora said.

"I do not understand." Malus raised one eyebrow.

"To maintain control of the entire nation of Vlada Children's Army, there needs to be punishment to those that do not follow your law," Gora added. "I suggest you practice these new methods."

"An example please."

"Three pigs go missing. The farmer finds his pigs on a neighbor's plot. He goes to the neighbor and asks for his pigs. If the neighbor agrees, nothing happens. But, if the neighbor challenges the farmer, you must interrogate the farmer, the neighbor and inspect the pigs. You pass your judgment, which produces consequences if it is not completed." Gora paused.

"What is different?"

Excellent. He will be easy to mold. "Your demeanor must be firm and free of prejudice; and, the action followed up to insure your judgment is enforced. You should practice so you will be ready at the critical early stages after our invasion. A good method to start with is to deny any changes and make the two people figure out the solution. You will start to see how people's minds work. Once you are comfortable you can issue a law."

"Okay I will give it a try," Malus replied.

There, the demise of Malus is set up. The orphans will be frustrated because Malus will decide the complaints one at a time.

He will have multiple answers to similar problems, which creates jealousy and higher anxiety. With a gentle push from me, Malus's leadership will not satisfy the leaders within the horde. The orphans unity will crumble. Hatred of Malus will grow as they approach Manshire. The dream of their new home will be more powerful for they will become more emotionally attached to what is left of their goals. By the time the orphans figure out what has happened Manshire will be destroyed and I will live again in Cyphera, perhaps Saraton.

Hauling Dragons

"Phyer is this way." Madison pointed. Kendrick's limp hindered his ability to keep pace with Madison's youthful legs.

"How is that arm?" Kendrick asked, hoping he would stop to talk about it.

"Sore. The corpsmen said it was not broken." Madison did not stop or look over his shoulder; however, his enthusiasm and stride increased when he talked of the dragon. "You will like him. He is smart—a quick student. Just a little further." Madison leaned forward as if walking against the wind.

"How is he going to react being covered in the wagon? Will he be okay riding for nine hours?" Kendrick asked.

"He is in here," Madison said.

Kendrick could see twenty-feet into the cave, but no dragon. "Madison, did you hear my questions?"

"I do not know how to answer. Richard use to say 'we will learn together'."

Kendrick turned the corner at twenty-five feet. A quick movement in the dark caught his attention—two gold eyes stared down at him. Immediately he had memories of his dragon—the wild ride, stabbing the sword into its head, felling the beast with two tiny arrows and the hard landing. *I hope Phyer cannot read my mind.* He heard a soft snort. Maybe a sneeze?

Madison walked past Kendrick and reached up to touch the pup's short arm. "You are making him nervous. Maybe he will settle down if he can see all of you."

The situation had become crazy. His son was bonding with the earth's lone dragon. He and Oscar had hoped to assassinate a few men, then escape a posse of several thousand warriors. Ultimately, finding the invasion force had been children—not exactly an acceptable target.

How is Phyer going to react to thousands of screaming sword-wielding orphans? What has our son done to deserve this risky and unique task?

Outside the cave the introductions began: "Father, meet Phyer. Phyer, my father, Kendrick...Watch, Father."

"Sedere." The dragon sat.

"Ascensorem." Phyer bent over and Madison climbed onto the dragon's neck.

"Sto." The eight-foot pup stood up.

Kendrick's eyes opened wide, the same size as Phyer's. His head tilted back as Madison ten plus feet in the air sat on Phyer's shoulders. The dragon was not even full-grown; his feet and head seemed too large for the legs and neck.

"Denuo." Phyer lowered his head to the ground for Madison to step off.

"Cover your ears," Madison said. "Loqui." A loud rumbling roar shook the ground.

"Why are the commands in Latin?" Kendrick asked.

"To prevent the enemy from controlling Phyer," Madison replied.

"Does he fly with you riding?"

"Not yet, but he can carry a bag of rocks three quarters of my weight."

"I am very impressed, Madison. You are doing a great job of training and bonding with Phyer." He smiled. It felt good praising his son for a job well done.

The sergeant's corpsmen were struggling to remove a bookshelf through the awkward door. *They will be at least an hour.*

"Madison, is that meadow still below the cliff?"

"Yes, and Phyer has kept the grass short—he eats there from time to time."

Kendrick and Madison walked down the road to the meadow. Madison suggested they sit on the big rocks lining the shore.

Madison looked up at him quizzically. "Why were you gone for so long?"

"This is between you and me. Understand?"

"Most certainly, Father."

"Twelve years ago, a few weeks before your birth, your mother and I had similar visions about an invasion. A few days later Richard arrived at the castle...his predictions came true...we have tried to find solutions that did not require you to fly Phyer...your grandpa and I went to the frontier to disperse the horde..."

A large shadow swept over them. Kendrick's heart sank as he watched Phyer fly out over the ocean.

"Do not worry, it is his training time. He will be back in five minutes," Madison said. "Please tell me the rest of the story."

"We expected to find thousands of marauders marching toward Manshire...we split up to gather information faster...Oscar was spotted by an old enemy." Far off in the sky Kendrick saw a growing speck, "Is that Phyer?"

"See, I told you. Watch this," Madison stood and circled his fist overhead.

Phyer's wings beat faster as he focused on Madison. Phyer landed in the meadow and began to graze on the knee-high grasses at the base of the cliff.

A whistle came from the cliff above. A corpsman swung his arm three times from his side to over his head. Phyer kept eating.

"We must be ready to go."

Madison moved his arm straight in front of him. Phyer flew off the meadow, circled twice, then disappeared past the cliff's edge. "He will be waiting for us."

"What is in those four books?" Kendrick asked as they climbed the steep trail.

"Poems, drawings, notes, journal like entries and diagrams of the sun with shadowed balls. And some weird letters, X, I, V, on calendars. June twenty-first is circled several times—my birthday."

->>><<<-

Regardless of how the wagon was loaded, one of Phyer's limbs remained uncovered. Other solutions had various limitations—Phyer could not walk for nine miles and his size prohibited a disguise.

"Madison, will Phyer follow you regardless of where you are?" Kendrick asked.

"I believe so. No one rides him now."

Kendrick turned to the corpsman. "If we take eight Long Bows and ride as fast as the horses will go. Madison can give hand commands. Three Caves will be about four hours. Leaving at dawn, we might arrive before the roads get too busy,"

Kendrick paced most of the night. A few times he stopped to enjoy his son's peaceful sleep. In another hour, they would be racing along back roads hoping no one saw the dragon, or his gifted son.

He looked east waiting for the first stars to extinguish their sparkle for the daytime.

"Madison, time to depart."

"Can I sleep five more minutes?" Madison mumbled. He laid his head on the rolled up blanket.

"Sure, but the corpsman needs your *pillow* to cover the books in the wagon."

"Okay, I will get up," Madison replied.

"Wake the dragon. Do you think there is enough light for Phyer?"

"Richard had us train in the evenings twice a week," Madison replied.

Ten minutes passed before Madison exited the cave with Phyer.

"Are we at risk if some farmer accidently uses a visual command?" Kendrick asked.

"I am not sure, but I have been the only one to use hand signals."

"Your hand stretched out straight in front of you like before?"

"Yes, just like that, Father."

As Kendrick completed the hand command. Phyer tilted his head.

"Now you do it," Kendrick said.

Phyer spread his wings and was airborne in two steps.

"Excellent. You are with me, Madison." Kendrick helped his son onto the saddle. "Two Long Bows ride ahead. We do not need any surprises today."

The first three hours went as planned. Anytime eye contact with Madison was interrupted, Phyer circled.

Suddenly, a corpsman approached them slapping the horse's back with the reins. At twenty feet he tugged the reins to stop the horse. "A couple of wagons coming this way."

"Give the signal to land as soon as you can." They rode for a quarter mile before Madison could see Phyer. He circled his fist above his head until Phyer started to descend. Kendrick pointed to the sergeant who nodded, then ordered his men to hide. Three minutes later they found Phyer munching on some berry bushes at the side of the road. "Madison we have to hide our dragon."

Kendrick placed a palm against his forehead. *Walking dragons are the slowest creatures...*

"I will ride ahead to stall them."

Approaching the first of two wagons, Kendrick tried to smile easily, though his heart pounded. There was a driver up front and a passenger riding in the wagon . The wagon's load was concealed under blankets and ropes.

The driver pulled on the reins stopping the horses. "Did you see that thing flying in the sky?" he asked. "It was huge."

"No, you are the first I have seen this morning. Where are you headed?"

"Moving back to help my father. His brother has died and we will be working the farm. Did you not see the big bird?" The man looked up. Fortunately, the skies were clear.

"Sorry," Kendrick offered, hoping his laid back demeanor told the man all.

"We were afraid it was circling to attack us," the driver said. "But if you didn't see anything, perhaps I have been on the road too long."

Kendrick looked at the passenger. The man's eyes were large and he was holding onto the rope with fierceness, though he said nothing.

"We should be moving on. A long road ahead."

The driver slapped the reins and the wagon jerked forward. The man and boy on the second wagon waved as they passed. Their load was also covered with blankets and ropes.

Waiting on the first wagon, in its stalled position a bit of blood the size of a man's palm had formed under the second wagon. Had they kept moving, Kendrick would not have detected the individual drops. He reached for his bow. *Flaming dragons. I cannot help with this dysfunctional hand.*

He followed the wagons to the area hiding the Long Bows.

"Check the loads," Kendrick ordered.

The wagons halted.

"We are the queen's hunters and have gathered this meat for a festival," the driver said. "You have no right to stop us."

Pulling the covers back revealed animal trophy heads—an elk had fresh blood dripping from its neck.

"You are the queen's hunters?" Kendrick asked. "Not returning to help your father?"

"Yes."

"Sergeant, please send four Long Bows to protect our charge." Kendrick said and then turned to the driver. "I am Prince Kendrick, Duke of Manshire. You are under arrest."

The driver slapped the reins and bolted up the road. The second wagon quickly followed.

"You four! Go with Kendrick to protect Prince Madison. The rest, with me to capture the wagons!" the sergeant shouted.

Kendrick was about to speak when a large swift shadow darkened the ground next to him. Madison was riding Phyer! Kendrick extended his fist into the air and circled it three times— He was not sure if Madison saw him. "Follow the dragon!" he commanded, his thoughts a jumble of anxiety and pride.

"Ignis, Ignis!" Two fireballs hurled from Phyer's mouth. The four bandits leapt from the wagons, one trying to remove burning clothes, the other rolling on the ground.

The Long Bow Knights circled the four riders. Kendrick arrived and proceeded to the four men lined beside the second wagon. These men had been hunting for quite a while, as Kendrick could smell them over the stench of burning trophy head hair.

Kendrick took his knife, scraping elk blood from the wagon's planks. He wiped a spot of blood onto each bandit's shirt over the heart.

"Sergeant, will one knight per prisoner be sufficient to hit these targets?" Kendrick asked, repositioning the corpsmen. He pointed to the red spot on the nearest bandit's shirt.

"Most certain, sir." The corpsmen prepared arrows.

"Who is the leader of this band of criminals?" Kendrick asked. Three of the four bandits looked to the one with the blue shirt. "You must be a democracy. They voted for you."

"So?" asked Blue-shirt.

"This is what you can expect from me—an arrow, or two, for each wrong answer. I will decide on the value of the question. And, in fairness, I will tell you the value before I ask. Is that fair?"

"NO," blurted Blue-shirt.

"It was a bogus question. I just wanted you to think I was fair," Kendrick smiled as he faced the corpsmen and tapped his left arm before returning his attention to the bandits. "You with the red hat—are you his son?"

"We are all sons. I am the youngest," Red-hat said as he proudly smiled at his answer.

"Interesting. That puts a different reflection on this interrogation. Who is the oldest son?" Three of the four stared at the bearded bandit.

"For one arrow, are you really the queen's hunters?" Kendrick asked, hoping they'd get comfortable answering questions.

"No, sir," said the oldest son, producing a light whistle as he exhaled.

"I feel I should inform you that I was the hunter for my family. For one arrow, when did you kill the elk?" Kendrick asked. He pointed to the thin son.

"This morning, about an hour before we met you, Prince Kendrick," Thin-son replied.

"Okay Blue-shirt, you have raised three honest boys. I hope you are a good example. Why were you travelling toward upper Manshire Province?"

"To sell trophy heads to the queen," Blue-shirt said.

Kendrick placed one finger above his shoulder. A corpsman shot Blue-shirt in the arm on the opposite side of the bloodstain. Blue-shirt groaned and bent over at the waist. He was breathing heavily when he stood.

"Let this be a warning. I am quite capable of knowing a lie." Kendrick said. He limped past the bandits slowly swinging his cane and found what he wanted—Thin-son was sweating.

"Middle son, why were you traveling toward upper Manshire Province? But before you answer, if you lie both you and your father will die." He'd silently counted to thirty-five seconds before Blue-shirt broke the silence.

"Darell, tell him!"

"Yes, Father. We were trying to find the young prince to use his calming powers on herds of wildlife."

"You were planning to kidnap the young prince?"

"Yes." A collective sigh exhaled from the father and three sons.

"Sergeant, have some corpsmen take these four to prison then return to our destination."

Red-hat made a fist and prepared to slug his father. A corpsman shot an arrow between them that stuck in the wagon's sideboard. The fist relaxed, but his voice hardened, "I told you to kill the dragon. Who else besides the royal family would have a son riding a dragon? Your stupidity put us in prison."

The sergeant approached Kendrick. "Do you want them spreading the story of the prince and dragon?"he whispered.

"Place them away from the other prisoners. Thank you."

Kendrick walked toward Madison. Though there had been no blood shed—this time—there was no denying Madison's secret was no longer a secret.

->>><<<-

In the foothills, a half-day's ride from the Manshire castle, was a warm water cave, a large open cave room and a forty-foot dry cool cave named Three Caves. A moat like ring of two to five inch igneous rocks circled the cave complex for a mile in any direction making entry slow and dangerous.

"Sergeant, Madison will have authority regarding Phyer's wellbeing and training. Madison, the sergeant has authority over safety concerns," Kendrick said. "We will need to be prepared for battle on June twenty-first—eleven months from now."

"Kendrick sir. My other men?" the sergeant asked.

"I will send them all here. Madison's safety and security is your primary objective."

"Understood."

Leaning on his walking stick, Kendrick took a few deep breaths and looked to the sky. "We will need to develop our battle plans. I will arrange those meetings. Madison, allow some time each day to train with the sergeant. It would be prudent for you to be skilled with arrow, sword and knife."

"Yes, Father."

The ribbon was white.

At Home

Kendrick rode alone for five hours. Enjoying the end of summer he was passed by wagons abundantly filled with harvested goods going to market. The smell of fresh unearthed potatoes and carrots momentarily sent him back to a simpler time at the market, where he had first met Althea. Kendrick knew he had been gone to long...

He carried Oscar's weapons and tied his to the saddle. Uncertain why, he felt safer being close to Oscar's weapons, though he was unable to use them. Triggered by a glimpse of the castle through a break in the trees, memories of combat, battles and conflicts flooded his mind

His neck muscles tightened. Seconds later his back muscles constricted and his breathing grew labored. He dismounted and walked to the road's edge. To keep from falling he knelt on one knee. *I am going to faint. No!* He lowered his head, closed his eyes and pictured Althea. Two deep breaths later he felt better.

Kendrick looked at himself in the smooth pools beside the road. His long hair framed his face along with a shabby beard. The constant exposure to the sun and snow had tanned his wrinkled, lined face. *I almost did not recognize me.*

He needed time to think.

Kendrick walked the horse the last half-mile, through the market area, between the castle and cathedral and tied it to the post at the main entrance. A young Long Bow recruit was resting there.

If he sneezes the bow will fall to the ground. I wonder if someone has taught him how to dress? His weapon's belt needs

adjustment to stop his sword from rubbing on the ground. You should be standing—people will better respect your authority.

The recruit must have sensed his presence. "Sorry, but you cannot tie your horse here," the young Long Bow recruit, began, standing stiffly in front of him..

You have to be the shortest Long Bow ever. "Where shall I tie it?" *He really is quite muscular.* Kendrick stroked his beard.

"You could try the stables. Go up this street and turn left just past the gate. Or, the blacksmith at the end of the market area." When the lad pointed, his bow slipped off the other shoulder.

"Thank you. Can I leave the horse tied here?"

"Sorry sir, we are expecting Oscar and Kendrick to return soon."

"I am certain they will not mind if I use the post for a short while." A smile raised the corners of his mouth.

"Queen Althea has ordered the next horse to hitch here must be one of theirs."

Zachery, the Captain of The Long Bows, exited the castle. He stopped for a moment and peered over at him. "Is that you Kendrick?! I almost did not recognize you with that beard. Nice to see you. Why a walking stick?"

"Broke my leg in the frontier. It is only temporary, I hope."

"Queen Althea is in the assembly hall reviewing plans to defend the castle," Zachary said as he glanced at Kendrick. "We can get together later. You have got to tell me everything. Where is Oscar?"

"I buried him by Mother."

"Forgive me, I did not know. He was a great man."

"Yes. A great man." Kendrick's eyes shifted to the scene behind Zachery, one in which he was more than anxious about. Sweat formed on his back.

He looked at Zachary. "The queen awaits."

The boy blushed. "Yes...she will be happy to see you,"

Kendrick gripped Zachery's forearm. They shook hands.

Kendrick turned and extended his hand to the other red faced recruit. "I am Kendrick and you are?"

"Simon, Peter Simon, sir." They shook hands. "Welcome back to Manshire, sir."

Peter held the large oak door open and Kendrick walked down the hallway. He could smell the hint of cinnamon, which triggered thoughts of the second meeting with Althea near the big oak. A sense of belonging drifted gently through his being like a sailboat gliding with the breeze. For the first time he noticed the slight echoing of his boots off the solid stonewalls and hard wood ceiling. *Perhaps Oscar's ghost is walking with me.*

A blue-green light reflected off Reginald's white shirt as he walked through the open assembly hall door. Reginald turned to check who was standing in the hall. Kendrick crossed a finger on his lips. Reginald stepped out, gave a quick handshake and whispered, "I am so glad to see you. She needs you...Why the cane?"

"It is nothing. A break that is almost healed."

"So good to see you. I will not take more of your time—you are not here to see me."

Along the far wall she stood, gripping the edge of the table, her back to the door. Before her was a map of Manshire castle with single miniature soldiers and little brown blocks.

"Reginald, can you give me a quick review of the new land laws?" Only the chatter of two crickets filled the silence. "Father?" Under her breath she said, "Humph, already gone."

Althea moved the small wood blocks around the castle drawing. Turning, she paced along the table. Upon reaching the bow and quiver at the table's end she lingered a few seconds, touching the quiver, then changed directions. Kendrick watched as her palm slowly massaged her chin, her brow pinched at the top of her nose.

The room tint darkened as her shadow passed through the light reflecting off the blue-green curtains and equally highlighted her shortened sandy blonde hair. She stopped, pointing her index finger as though she was recognizing God for the idea, her head tilted slightly, her eyebrows lifted. Leaning over the map she moved a few blocks.

"That helps," she said. taking a deep breath. "I wish Kendrick and Oscar were here."

154

"Your wish is granted!" Kendrick replied.

Time appeared to stop. He watched her stare at the ceiling as if receiving an answer from heaven. *Maybe she is wondering if I am a ghost, or perhaps she will not recognize me with this beard?*

"Kendrick!" She ran full speed toward him. Though he had dropped the walking stick, he managed to keep their balance during the embrace. He squeezed her tightly, "I missed—us. I love you more than I ever thought possible." The scent of her hair made his knees weak.

She kissed him.

Her hug loosened and she tilted her head back as she looked into his eyes. "Had to make sure it was you."

"Why do you say that?"

"You usually stop at *I love you.*" Tears highlighted the thousands of stars he saw in her bright blue eyes.

"I have a promise to keep with Bernard," he told her moments later.

"Bernard?"

"Let me tell you about the past six years." Kendrick held her hands. "We started at Manshire port and the port master actually provided some useful information. The frontier was truly vast. We lived off the land and talked to traders—Oscar was good at gathering information from the traders with a different language. We spent a day herding goats to get information from the herder. We stole clothes to blend in. Our eating and sleeping schedules were abandoned when we located the horde. Our focus to assassinate the leaders was lost when we discovered the marauders were children…"

Althea placed a hand over his mouth, the other hand over her lips and shook her head. "And they will be battling my son who will likely die. I wish we had never heard of marauders, ancient birds, or Richard," she said.

He stood, trying to hide the limp as he walked, mostly to hide his eyes from her, but his shaky voice gave away his struggle to say, "We were stoned by the marauders. Oscar knocked me to the ground and covered me during the first volley of stones that took his life."

Althea gasped. "How-how did you survive?"

"I had several broken bones. Bernard spent nine months helping me heal. He told me that Bernyce died the same day he became my doctor."

"What?"

"Bernard is an angel."

"What? Well, that explains why we could not find Bernyce."

"Our old enemy Argo calls himself Gora now. The large bear like man from our visions riding a black Clydesdale is Malus—he is probably the first orphan marauder. He and Argo, or Gora, do not get along well, but Gora has something that Malus wants, which might be the location of Manshire."

"After I buried Father, I traveled to Richard's and watched him die saving Madison," Kendrick said.

Althea looked to the floor and shook her head. "I misjudged him," she said.

"I am quite impressed by Madison's training with Phyer—."

"How is Madison? I receive a weekly report from the sergeant."

"He is well and very excited about working with the dragon and he found four books you and I should review. We successfully moved him to Three Caves where he is guarded by the sergeant and his corps."

"Why would you move him?" Althea asked.

"Hunters attempted to abduct Madison," Kendrick replied. "I have asked the sergeant to give our son some basic defense training."

"He is thirteen," Althea said.

"I was eleven when the farm duties were my responsibility."

"But, farm chores are not likely to surprise, attack and kill you," she replied.

"All the more reason for him to be prepared, because you never know when someone may attack," Kendrick replied. "Same logic as giving you archery lessons."

She stared at the ceiling like she was looking for a response to be written there. After a lengthy pause she sat up in the chair.

"I am an over protective mother—one that knows her son is likely to drown on his fourteenth birthday. I want to hug him every day."

She stared at the map, her arms folding on the table. Her eyes moved slowly from the map to Kendrick to the floor as she aimlessly twirled a wood block on the map. He waited for her to make eye contact.

"We might have a chance to survive the assault. But, we need a unique scheme to guarantee victory," Kendrick said.

"This is a lot of information. I need time to think."

"I want to find Roslyn," Kendrick said. "Walk with me?" He reached for her hand.

"Remember, she was very young when you left. She has few memories of you." Althea kissed his cheek and whispered, "Good to have you back.

They walked by her stepmother's rugs, the statue of her stepfather and a painting of her.

"Nice addition to the gallery," Kendrick said. They walked to the end of the hall.

"Here is the playroom." Roslyn was drawing a young tree with several large knots.

"Roslyn, how is your day?" Althea asked.

Roslyn remained focused on the drawing. "It is very good. I had a dream that Father would be home soon."

"Sooner than you might think," Kendrick said, dropping to one knee.

She dropped the pencil and looked up at him. "Father? But my father does not have a beard." Her mouth pouted her displeasure.

"If you give me a hug, I will shave the beard off and then you shall see. Can sit together at supper?" Kendrick asked.

"Uhhh...okay..."

He reached forth his arms.

The Apothecary

Additlene was wine country with rolling hills of grapevines. A cool, dry breeze protected the grapes that produced a bold, dry black wine. Gora remembered sharing a bottle with Lieutenant Cromwell when he had sent the ransom letter to Manshire.

The orphans' arrival could not have been better timed as Gora's small meetings with the horde's unofficial *rogue leaders,* soon to become *combatants*, started to make Malus visibly uneasy. Returning from one such meeting, Gora walked by Malus's tent and heard, "As we get closer to our journey's end, the valley of our distrust widens by the day and the need to keep him will be questionable. Vee, spend more time with him so we can determine if he is truly a concern," Malus had said.

Gora estimated the journey would end in about five months—the days he would use to work his control of Vee. Since *accompanying* the Vlada Orphan Army he had abstained and missed wine. The next step in his plan required an introduction of wine into Vee's diet. But first he needed to find an apothecary.

Walking a half-mile to the village gave Gora time to review the mixture he needed to redirect Vee's loyalty—the potion must be tasteless and create a dire dependence.

Gora recalled his father saying, *if you want to find someone, ask his advisory.*

A conversation with the priest had revealed the location of an apothecary. To his surprise the two-mile walk went by quickly for his mind was busy plotting Vee's special handling.

The house fit the priest's description exactly. A five-foot section of fencing was attached to each side of the gate and followed the road's curve. Oddly, no other fencing enclosed the front yard.

At the priest's suggestion Gora stopped at the gate and yelled to the house, "Stafford, are you in there?"

"Who wants to know?" came the reply.

"A friend seeking help for a comrade," Gora replied.

"Enter."

Knee-deep grass lined the pea gravel path, which shifted and crunched with each of the forty steps to the house.

A pudgy five and a half foot man opened the door before Gora knocked. One white eye stared at the sky and a tattered patch covered the other.

"How can I help you?" Stafford asked.

"I need a potion to help a struggling friend caring for eleven young orphans that recently lost parents in a village fire. He will die if he does not rest occasionally. I am hoping you can make a tonic which I will administer allowing him to forget his troubles if only for a few hours a week. He cannot sleep, but hibernate like a bear," Gora said.

"Yes, it is possible. But, there are cautions."

Gora had used a similar potion once on a sister and knew the potential problems. He was counting on them.

"Please tell me."

"You will need to mix it with something like wine or ale. It tastes terrible in water. No more than two times per week—otherwise he will become highly dependent on you and nothing else. You must be careful to avoid breathing, touching, or swallowing the potion or you will suffer the same fate," Stafford warned.

"When will it be ready?"

"Two hours."

"And if I wanted to buy two portions?" Gora asked.

"I will make both at the same time."

->>><<<-

"It is time to go," Kendrick said. "Two knights disguised as Althea and I, with Simon Peter dressed as Roslyn, left about an hour ago. A Long Bow Knight returned saying the decoys were not followed."

"Are you sure you want to do this?" Althea asked.

"Yes."

"Kendrick, you have great instincts, why change what has been successful before our darkest hour?" Althea asked.

"This is a battle unlike any other," Kendrick replied. "Like other enemies they are armed and trained, but we cannot fight them using traditional methods."

Roslyn slept on the front seat of the black carriage. The worn leather was cracked with tufts of cotton poking through in a dozen locations. Dust swirled like the morning fog in the beams of sunlight and settled on their clothing. Occasionally the cabin, suspended on four thick leather straps, slammed into the framework as one of the bands had rotted in storage. Being the older of the two royal carriages, Kendrick thought his family would be safe in a coach with a common appearance.

Lifting the dusty grey curtain to establish their location took only a few seconds as Kendrick recognized the four short buttes named The Choir—less than thirty minutes to Three Caves.

The carriage stopped abruptly causing Kendrick to extend his arm to keep Roslyn on the seat.

"Is that Madison that I hear? Is he speaking Latin?" Althea asked.

"Yes," Kendrick said as he opened the door, stepped out and then assisted Althea from the cabin. He lifted Roslyn from the doorway and sat her on the ground then slid his hand gently over her dress to remove the dust.

"There. You are pretty again," Kendrick said. Roslyn held his hand as they walked to the large area central to the caves. The *whoosh* of Phyer's wings stirred up small whirlwinds of dust.

"Solum," Madison commanded. Phyer changed the angle of his wings and extended his feet a few seconds before he landed. A short snort expelled a mist as the dragon landed.

"They are so big." Althea placed her hands in front of her mouth and raised her eyebrows. Kendrick placed his hand in the middle of Althea's back and held Roslyn's hand as they crossed the field.

"Denuo." Phyer lowered his head to the ground for Madison to dismount.

The dragon was eleven feet tall. Greenish red scales covered most of his body, the neck covered with a thin coating of a sticky film. Seven horns protruded between the neck and head—three on each side surrounding the small ear holes and a single small one on the top of his head. Phyer's impressive feet were a bow's length by an arrow's width. Madison had once seen Phyer's tail swat a dog. When flying at night the gold eyes changed to red.

"Mother!" He ran to her open arms. Althea squeezed *her little man* tightly thinking that soon she would have the last hug from Madison.

"Do not worry. We will be successful," Madison said. Althea held him until he said, "Thank you, Mother."

He turned to Roslyn, hugged her, then winked. "Do you miss me at the castle?"

"You are gone?" she teased then pointed to Phyer. "He is big. You have command of this huge dragon?"

"Yes. Watch." Madison replied. "Sedere." Phyer sat. "Would you like to sit on him?"

Althea crossed her arms, cleared her throat to get Kendrick's attention and aimed her disapproving eyes at him.

"My queen." She knew he was about to offer a disagreeable point of view. "It is perfectly safe. Would you like to determine for yourself that it is safe for Roslyn?"

"Well done," she mouthed to Kendrick. She had no choice but to sit on Phyer or express her lack of confidence in this 'ancient bird' in front of Madison.

"Okay, I want to be sure this dragon is safe," said Althea.

"Ascensorem." Phyer lowered his head to the ground. Madison held her hand as he instructed, "Throw your right leg over his neck. Get ready—he is about to stand. Sto." She felt his hot breath on her legs. To her surprise the two horns she grabbed were smooth yet she had a firm grip. The full-grown dragon calmly lifted the queen eleven feet above the ground.

"Mother, pull the right horn." Phyer took several small steps to turn right. Althea smiled as she cautiously "Oooo'd" with each hitch in the movement.

161

"He is about to lower you. Denuo." The dragon slowly lowered her. "Release the horns before he reaches the ground, then he will lower his head so you can swing your leg over."

Althea was visibly shaking yet her big smile was true.

"Okay Roslyn, it's your turn," said Kendrick walking to Althea's side. He reached for her hand; she squeezed and then whispered, "Thank you. That was scary, but very exciting." She lifted their clasped hands and said, "Delightful to have you back."

Roslyn giggled nervously as Madison helped her mount Phyer. When the dragon lifted her, one hand went to her chest, possibly to keep her heart from jumping out. Laughter filled the immediate area with every movement. Her mouth fell open as Phyer lowered her. Dismounting she slid off and landed too close to Phyer's shoulder. The dragon leaned forward pushing Roslyn about a foot then stood up.

"Why, you have all the fun," a feisty Roslyn whispered, patting Madison on the cheek.

"Sergeant, is lunch ready?" Kendrick asked.

"Yes sir. Phyer's food cave is ready." The Sergeant glanced at Kendrick and lifted one finger. "It is the best cave. The dragon's cave has a most offensive odor and the other is hot and humid," the sergeant said nodding.

Queen Althea, Prince Kendrick of Manshire, Prince Madison heir apparent, Princess Roslyn and the sergeant walked to the cave. Roslyn was the first person through the opening. "Oh my. How much does he eat?"

"About two bundles a day," the sergeant answered. "About the same weight as Madison." Kendrick looked to Althea—she was staring at the floor shaking her head.

The sergeant continued, "We have three knights gathering food from dawn to dusk. I apologize the furniture and surroundings do not recognize your class. They are the best we could gather."

A large irregular six-sided grey flagstone sat on three large boulders. Four stools were cut from large diameter stumps—two for adults and two for children and a folded saddle blanket lay on each stool. A plate by each chair had grilled rabbit meat, carrots, roots and bread. The large cup held water.

162

"They are more than adequate for our needs. Thank you for your special efforts," replied Kendrick. He turned to Althea and offered the slightest of nods. "Please join us. We might need a soldier's point of view," Althea asked. "This is special and quite nice."

Kendrick began with a shortened version of their mission—Manshire port, Frontier, traders, horde's devastation, spying and being stoned. He paused and then revealed that the marauder warriors were children. The sergeant standing against the grey flagstone leaned over and rested his hands on the tabletop. Kendrick lifted his brows and nodded when the sergeant searched for validation.

"Children. I am not sure I could kill children," the sergeant said.

"Kendrick, you were right," Althea affirmed. *He is the knight we send on clandestine missions and we depend on him to kill if he deems it necessary.*

"Kendrick, sir, if I may be so bold, why did you let the leaders live?" the sergeant asked as he sat.

"The children are dependent on the leaders and removing them would be akin to killing the orphans," Kendrick replied.

The sergeant looked down at the tabletop then stood slowly. He crossed his arms. "What are we to do?"

"That is the purpose of this meeting," Althea said. "Kendrick has convinced me that our tactics must be different, bold and unexpected. We invited Madison and Roslyn to provide a variety of new options. We cannot order the kingdom to kill the child warriors if we are having a similar difficulty."

The sergeant looked at Kendrick's shaking left hand resting on the table. "Your hand was injured because you could not shoot the children stoning you?"

"Yes. Which confirms our need for a non-violent confrontation. We have a blend of several tactical objectives never considered—the leader must remain alive, a previous enemy is guiding the horde to Manshire and we are unsure what to do with thousands of orphans. We must prove this is the true end of the orphans' journey," Kendrick said.

"What happened when the orphans entered other villages?" Roslyn asked.

"Some villages were spared retaliation. Some burned to the ground," Kendrick replied. "The difference? How the resident orphans were treated."

"Why are they coming to Manshire?" Madison asked.

"We think Gora, whom we know as Argo, has convinced the leader, Malus, that Manshire is the place to settle for orphans. I suspect Gora has plans to eliminate Malus and order the horde to attack, hoping to finally extract his revenge on Manshire." Kendrick replied. "Gora is clever. He will have a backup plan. The village attacks were likely battle exercises."

Althea asked Madison to display Richard's four books on the table. "Kendrick and I reviewed these books. One explains and approximates the full eclipse at between 10:23 a.m. to 12:07 p.m. on June twenty-first. Two have various pieces of the prophecy and it appears the two together are like a puzzle starting with our visions nearly fourteen years ago. The last book, we have yet to determine its purpose. It has drawings without captions. Kendrick recognizes parts of drawings, but not the whole of the drawings."

Madison walked to the fourth book.

"Richard said this book is the prediction of what happens after the horde arrives at Manshire—he found it in an old church on the north shore. The priest died in his sleep before he could tell Richard how to read it," Madison explained.

"Kendrick and I are concerned as we have several interpretations to many of the drawings. Take this drawing for example: Are the orphans charging the castle or the ballista's? Or, this one with the large man being attended by a younger male both targeted by five archers."

The sergeant turned two pages then raised his eyebrows and pointed to a drawing. He asked, "What is the meaning of these twelve arrows stuck in the cross?"

"We are not sure. One assumption we are comfortable with is, the darker drawings take place during the eclipse—which is when Richard predicted the marauders would charge the castle," Kendrick said.

"But, this picture shows the castle being attacked after the eclipse," Althea added.

Eleven-year old Roslyn, took a drink, walked to the open book and began examining it at page one. Kendrick scratched his head and Althea replied with shrugged shoulders.

After five minutes, Roslyn closed the book. "I think this book contains two stories. And depending on choices made with the marauders, we or the marauders will reside in the castle at the end of the day."

"Show me what you found." Althea walked quickly to Roslyn as she pointed to the pages.

"Here on page one begins a series of five drawings without the squiggly line in the right or left corner. I think they tell of the two sides meeting. Then on page six, notice the drawings on the left have the squiggly line in the lower left corner and the right, in the lower right," Roslyn said.

"Good thinking. Do you have an interpretation for the two sets of drawings?" asked Kendrick.

She thumbed through the next seven pages with Althea looking over Roslyn's shoulder. Several minutes later she said, "The left pages show a big man being shot, then involved in a fight supported by the attending man. The armed men shown here are a third group that kill the big man and the attending man in a small battle. Madison arrives on Phyer, but he is too late. The orphans have taken over the castle. You can see where three pages have been torn out," Roslyn replied as she showed the remnants of the ripped pages.

"What is that?" Althea pointed at the second ripped page remnant.

"It reminds me of the angel carving grandfather gave me." Roslyn removed the necklace and set it beside the inked half image. Roslyn and Althea's eyes met then returned to the angel necklace and the remaining half drawing. Kendrick put his arm around Madison as they walked to book four.

"It makes sense when you *read* the drawings as she explains," said Althea.

Several minutes passed before she began. "See here... Father, Mother and I meet the leader of the orphans who only want a mother, a home and respect. Look! Their *mother* is represented by this figure here—it looks similar to Mother and the carving on top of Father's walking stick."

A quick check at the top of Kendrick's walking stick from Bernard leaning on the table tells them she is right.

"The leader is shot by a rogue archer and is near death," Roslyn continued. "I think these are the leader's guards aiming at Father. The next drawing has ink spilled on this corner, but it shows us, the leader and his guards involved in a battle against a third group inside a small building. Unfortunately, the last three pages are missing," said Roslyn.

Kendrick walked away from the table with both hands resting on his head. "It appears we die or are booted from the castle." He rubbed his shaved chin then walked outside the cave.

"Wait here. I want to talk with Kendrick alone," said Althea. She walked quickly to his side. "What is your thinking? I know you are not afraid of death or living off the land—you have faced both too many times."

"I may not be able to create a scheme that meets our needs. Previous schemes had factual information gathered by spying and interrogation. This scheme has to be based on future events from multiple disagreeing sources—our visions were similar yet different, the marauders are children not adults, the leaders are caregivers not commanders. Book four has multiple outcomes, Richard, who guessed a lot and poetry books with mysterious pages. I feel your frustration."

"*I would like to suggest you have all the knowledge needed to bring an acceptable conclusion to the invading orphan horde,*" Kendrick began, glancing at Althea—she was not speaking. "*You should think about taking paths that are unfamiliar, perhaps scary for you, or more risky than you are comfortable with.*"

"How did you *do* that?" Althea asked.

"I did nothing," Kendrick responded. "But those are Bernard's exact words from our conversation."

"*Trust what you know.*"

"There it is again," Althea said.

"Bernard?" Kendrick asked.

"*Yes. Believe your sense of right.*"

"We have been reacting to the visions, trying to outsmart Richard's predictions and looking for answers in old books with missing pages. I am struggling with this—*boxing match*. What is your response to creating our own schemes? Forget about the books, prophecies and Richard's yammering," Kendrick asked. "It is you and I plotting a course we prefer based on our knowledge and assumptions. Granted this situation is different, but we can adjust to the alterations."

"Yes!" Althea replied. She hugged him. "This is the Kendrick I know."

"Are you ready?"

"Most certainly."

->>><<<-

The sunset was a festival of colors that brought a sense of calm to Malus's troubled heart. His gaze slowly moved from the north to the south and back again, feeling calmer with each successive pass. When the colors had faded to night, Malus thought, *if we only knew where our home was located—I could be rid of Gora*. He felt rejuvenated and breathed deeply. He stood, smiled, lifted his shoulders and straightened his back. *I can try. If he says no, I have lost nothing.*

Striding through camp he found Gora drinking from one of his black bottles.

"Join me," Gora slurred holding up the bottle of wine.

Malus saw the two corks on the ground, which meant Gora was fully drunk. Gora took a big swig.

"Thank you," Malus offered." Did you see the sunset?"

"Yah. Check the fire—same colors and you can look at it anytime."

The black wine dyed the creases of his mouth. Malus knew that meant he had been drinking in frequent, fast gulps.

Malus took the bottle when it was offered again and shuttered before the bottle touched his lips. Sticking his tongue in the hole to stop the flow of wine, he exaggerated his swallowing as he handed the bottle back to Gora.

"How far are we from our new home? I am trying to plan for food and water rationing for early spring," Malus asked.

"Let me think. A month for boats, two weeks...across Estmira, a week to fight," Gora mumbled. He took another sloppy swig that dripped off his chin onto his shirt. "Shhh, do not tell anyone. Maybe seven months," he whispered.

"A week to fight seems like a lot. None of our battles have lasted more than a day," said Malus angrily, hoping to challenge Gora's ego.

"That is because you do not know Queen Althea, Kendrick and Oscar. They are a formidable team and you are a weak minded Auroch without my advice and experience." Gora's voice grew louder with each word. "I am told she is quite pretty and I can attest to her cleverness. Oscar is an aging knight with impeccable skills and thought. Kendrick, his son, is a younger version of Oscar and should not be underestimated." Gora's head slowly tilted forward until his chin rested on his chest, then jerked up as his eyes opened wide.

->>><<<-

Gora had been using the boat construction as a means of gaining back some of Malus's trust. He had answered every question regarding his woodcraft skills with, "it is wood and it will float." Fifteen one-foot diameter logs lashed together with rope taken in raids of the last five villages were assembled to create a bow. On the perimeter an extra log was tied on top as a railing.

The initial test was a disaster. The horse and nineteen of twenty orphans had survived, the crates of supplies, had floated for a few minutes then sunk.

Malus's face turned crimson and his breathing a series of short gasps, when he heard the twentieth orphan was found a half-mile down the beach with a large cut in her head.

"How could you be so stupid?" Malus released his rage a few inches from Gora's face. This was the first time since Vlada he had wanted to kill someone he knew. He clinched his fists.

"Stop!" Gora replied. "Who knew the horse would be sea sick and shift his weight?"

"You are banished from the army. You may have the wagon and its contents. I do not want to see you ever again," Malus's shoulders lifted slightly, he relaxed his hands. *That felt good. Of course, it had become easier because he had given away the location and directions to Manshire last night. Perhaps I should have helped him get drunk a month ago.*

"I hold the keys to Manshire, you will never find it without me," Gora insisted as he pressed his palms next to this temples.

"Did you forget your drunken tempest when you compared me to a slow untamed cow? I remember the words you used 'you are a weak minded Auroch?'" Malus's confidence grew every second—he no longer feared life without Gora. "We are clever enough to find Manshire from here. Goodbye," he said with a smile and for his own satisfaction added, "Remember to be gone before I wake tomorrow."

Malus backed away from Gora until they were several sword lengths apart. He scanned the crowd for Vee. "You four, find Vee and have him see me."

->>><<<-

In the gap between the army and leaders, Gora waited for Vee. The wait was short. He grabbed Vee's arm as he ran by the bush where Gora hid.

"Vee, gather the rogue leaders for a meeting. I think the stress of this journey has finally possessed him. If we are to successfully take over Manshire we will need to replace Malus," Gora said.

"I do not think I can do this anymore," Vee said. "Can you give me enough potion to sleep forever?"

"You will do as I require or do without the sleep aid. You must leave with me, or face Malus alone," Gora said.

Vee raised his fists above his head, spun slowly and pounded the air like he was beating a drum. A weak groan, from a man in agony with his rampant addiction versus his loyalty to an old friend, accompanied Vee's wild dance. Without notice, Vee grabbed his bow and quiver and ran away.

Desperation

May was rainy which added to   Malus's frustration. Gora's one week as boat construction leader had thoroughly impeded the progress as all the logs had been cut preventing any alterations to the design.

For twenty-one days, seven small wooden barges fitted with outriggers carried orphans, food, supplies and meager possessions across the narrowest part of the ocean. After two days of crossings, the rafts had to be repaired and ropes tightened.

Vee shook constantly. Malus thought it was the cold rain, but on clear days his behavior remained unchanged. Vee's moaning during the night reminded Malus of the wounded lying in a battlefield crying for help.

Malus spent a lot of time walking the beach watching the boats leave for Estmira and thinking about Gora.

->>><<<-

Twelve rogue leaders had gathered with Gora behind the goatherd as directed by Vee. Several leaders said Vee had gone to Malus's tent.

"Let me be quick, this could be a set-up," Gora said. He did not make eye contact, but kept scanning the area for Malus trusted guards. "In two weeks I will secretly rejoin the army to talk with you about plans to overthrow Manshire. I know them and they will fight to the end."

->>><<<-

Gora heard grass crunching and walked quickly away from the goatherd. He had travelled twenty feet when Vee appeared from the bushes. Gora pulled his knife.

"Careful with that. I come in peace," Vee said as he held up his hands. I thought we needed a spy in   Malus's camp. How about some of that sleeping aid?"

Battle for Mother

He walked into their chambers as she placed the coat on the bed. Her bright blue eyes fixed on him as he winked to her, but she saw his doubt in the wrinkles around his weary eyes.

"Good morning, my beautiful queen."

The past five years had been hard on her beloved husband. Since his father's death, he had become a bit reclusive in affairs of state, yet more loving to the children and attentive to her. She knew inside he was analyzing the details of his latest plan hoping to find a niche in his scheme—a niche that kept her, Roslyn and Madison off the battlefield.

The success of this scheme relied on a marginally predictable eclipse, Kendrick's undeveloped gift, a ghost's assurances, projecting a family image and Uncle Richard—a dead mystic and did not include the battle skills Kendrick had mastered.

"Good morning my handsome prince." In sixteen years of marriage she still felt awkward calling him prince, for she thought it belittling, but king was improper.

He approached with a hand behind his back. But, as before, the fragrance had entered the room before him. He handed her a single Amherst rose, his gift before each threatening mission or long separation. Althea so wanted the moment that came between him looking into her eyes and the *I-love-you* that followed, to linger a little longer.

As if he knew her mind, the kiss was longer than a moment and the warmth of his lips kindled her courage for this morning's agenda.

The horde was waiting.

->>><<<-

From the watchtower two hours later, Queen Althea and Prince Kendrick could see the treetops poking through the thick fog that had drifted in after the rain. It was eerie. Roslyn, two knights, Kendrick and Althea were the only occupants of the castle. A sneeze or cough covered the murmur of the fog-covered horde—it seemed the fog was sick. By this hour on any normal foggy day, the haze had cleared the castle and surrounding ward, yet the castle appeared to be smoking as the stubborn mist resisted evacuation.

The delayed fog worried Althea. The eclipse might be viewed as clouds moving in above the fog.

"It is time to go," she said to her princess.

They walked down the tower stairs, adjusted their clothes and then proceeded through the mist-covered gate.

"Is the horde louder?" Roslyn asked. She looked up to her mother's eyes. "I am scared."

Kendrick reached for Althea's hand.

"Me, too," Althea replied. "But, I believe in and am comforted by your father's scheme."

A few steps later they exited the mist surrounding the castle. Wearing a full-length ochre hooded hare coat on her shoulders, it was far from blending into the foliage for the first day of summer, but she hoped the horde's orphaned boys would hesitate when they saw *mother* in their sights.

Walking across the outer ward, the wind had not arrived. Althea's hopes for her hair to blow in the wind, matching the image described by Oscar to Kendrick, were dashed. Samantha had agreed to cut her hair and weave it to lengthen Althea's short hair. There was, however, a noticeable unsteady decrease in the murmur of the horde that had a calming effect on Roslyn and Althea hoped it meant the same for the horde.

Kendrick picked up Roslyn, winked to Althea and held her hand as they approached the meeting benches.

Benches made from large logs formed a square surrounding the fire pit. Kendrick let Roslyn walk between the log ends, stepped aside for Althea to enter, waived to a pair of knights with torches, then sat next to his wife.

The minutes seemed like days as the horde leaders did not leave the fog until the torchbearers had returned to the castle gate.

"That must be Malus?" Althea lowered her gaze and closed her eyes when she saw his face.

"True. The sickly one is his aid. I do not know the others," Kendrick replied.

"Where is Gora?"

"Good question."

"What is wrong with his face?" Roslyn whispered as she sat between Althea and Kendrick.

"Oscar thought he had been abused as a child. The swelling has a boxer's appearance with larger bumps, birth defects usually are smaller and more dense," Kendrick replied.

When Malus approached the opening, Althea, Kendrick and Roslyn walked toward him.

"I see you were expecting us." Malus pointed. "Fresh cut logs and fire pit rocks without ash residue...and my spies tell me the village is empty."

"Yes, we wanted your welcome to be special. I am Prince Kendrick, Duke of Manshire," Kendrick said. "I would like to introduce Althea Queen of Manshire and our daughter, Princess Roslyn. Our son, Prince Madison, will join us later."

Malus extended his hand to Roslyn. She smiled as his large paw swallowed her tiny hand. "You are very pretty. It is good that you look like your mother."

He stood in front of Kendrick and looked him in the eye with his hands clasped behind his back. "You and I know of each other. Gora told me perhaps too much on his last day with us. You and I may be too much warrior." Malus stared ahead for a few seconds, then looked at the ground around Kendrick.

"Your weapons?"

"They are behind this log. Placed here before dawn. My hope is that they will not be needed today."

Malus nodded once, then moved to Althea. He stared at her for what seemed like several minutes.

"Gora had little to say about you. But emphasized you were quite clever and determined for a woman. I am very pleased to meet the *Mother* of my orphans. I see you are wearing your bow and quiver." Malus removed his hat then bowed. She waited for him to stand.

"So that I may protect my daughter."

"Very good." He looked into their eyes one at a time. "You have a plan you wish to convey. Let us not waste these logs and fire." Malus crossed his arms. "But, I must tell you I am inclined to attack and take your castle." He sat on the log next to Althea. "Please begin."

Across the fire, Kendrick could see the five *delegate* guards had removed their bows and held an arrow.

"I feel a need to talk about Gora for we have a disconcerting history with him and need you to be aware of his clever nature," Kendrick said.

"I have a sense for Gora. He is quite the magician—what you see is only part of the trick. But continue," Malus said as he looked across the fire where Vee was sitting.

"Fifteen years ago he kidnapped twin girls to create a diversion while he kidnapped the queen later in the day. He lured my father to a negotiation with plans of also bargaining his life so he could destroy Manshire."

Malus began a slow walk around the fire.

"Your father would be Oscar?" he asked, scratching his beard.

Kendrick lifted his brow and turned his head slightly.

"Sorry that he died. I think I would have liked him," Malus added. "Let me assure you I have no plans to destroy Manshire. It is our destination—our home. But I will not release my leadership to someone I do not know. Unlike Gora, I prefer this 'battle' be an agreement of sorts; but I have thousands of warriors in this forest who are anxious to take Manshire by force if your negotiations are not sincere."

In that moment the deadly whisper of an arrow's flight ended in Malus's left lung above the heart. Kendrick pushed Althea and Roslyn to the ground much like Oscar protecting him from the stones. Though he missed his father every day, he was thankful to be available to protect his wife and daughter.

"Are you and Roslyn okay?" Kendrick asked. *What else can go wrong?*

"Yes," Althea answered, pointing to Malus. "Protect him."

Suddenly, an arrow whisked in their direction. It soared through the trees, it's point of origin the river near the castle, Five horde warriors moved into position. Kendrick slipped quickly between two guards. and as if he'd just tackled a true trunk, forced Malus to the ground. The tackle whisked up clouds of dust—further extending the pain in Kendrick's lung.

Vee fled toward the forest.

Checking on Roslyn, Kendrick found Althea had moved her against the large log, his eyes opening wide when she removed an arrow from her quiver. Heartache enveloped his soul.

"Sorry, Malus. Are you okay?" he asked.

I should have hidden a few Long Bow Knights.

"I am in pain and feel I may faint," came the quick reply.

"Is this the first time you have ever been shot?" *The arrow is above the heart. Why is his color changing so fast?*

"Yes."

Battlefield panic from first wounds.

The trampled grass made a perfect canvas for the five guards' shadows—without lifting his head Kendrick knew he was the target for five arrows and Althea was out numbered. He had to gain control quickly. He checked Malus's color—his cheeks were less grey and whiter. The white part of his eyes had a pearl appearance.

"Focus your mind on something pleasant like a house and land in Manshire. You will be okay," Kendrick said loud enough for the five warriors to hear. He patted Malus's good shoulder.

"Can you get me to the cathedral before I die?" Malus asked.

"Stop talking about dying," Kendrick said. He noticed the irritation in his own voice. "I promise to get you to the cathedral after we care for that wound."

"Please. I ask you to take me straight away to the cathedral."

"Can you order your guards to lower their weapons?" Kendrick asked.

"Yes, yes," Malus replied. He ordered the five warriors to stow their weapons. "I will be okay, wait in the forest for me. Be patient, as these things never happen as planned. Go amongst the army and communicate that they wait for my return."

"Might I suggest that two guards stay with you?" Kendrick asked.

"Good. Yes," Malus replied. "You two...with me."

"How is he?" Althea inquired.

"He is going to be fine," Kendrick replied. She knew that 'fine' meant *unsure*.

"We are in trouble if he dies!" she whispered.

We may have serious problems regardless. He glanced at the sun—a sliver along the right side had turned dark—time would be the new enemy. Caring for Malus would take a minimum of five minutes plus another ten minutes to honor his cathedral request.

Looking over his shoulder Kendrick saw one black and two grey ribbons. He had seen a lot of black single ribbons warning of danger. However, this was the first vision of two grey ribbons. He could only conclude they were less serious than three grey signifying a life of pain.

Kendrick picked up his weapons and signaled the two knights at the castle gate, ordering them to check the cathedral and wait.

Four minutes later, at the cathedral entry, Althea ordered the two knights to escort Roslyn into the empty castle.

Another action not part of our scheme. Worry filled Kendrick's soul.

"Are you sure? I think you should be with Roslyn," he said.

"She is safe. Nowhere in our visions, books, or poems does it mention Roslyn in danger. I want to help protect Malus." Kendrick knew when to argue with his wife, or bow to the queen's commands. It was a bowing moment.

Good. A pink ribbon—healing.

"Any idea who might want to kill Malus?" Althea asked.

"Two names come to mind," Kendrick replied.

->>><<<-

Malus lay near the center aisle on two oak benches shoved together just four rows from the altar—his hands clenched as he offered a prayer. Kendrick assumed the gesture was remembered from the orphanage.

Dear Lord. Thank you for blessing us with a safe arrival at our new home. We ask that you protect Manshire from attack. Please forgive the destruction and death we created along our long journey. I ask that you bless Kendrick that I may trust his words. If it be your will, help me live to see my orphans' dream come true. This is my prayer, amen."

He lowered his hands to his chest just as Kendrick appeared with a knife.

"Malus, I think we should remove that arrow, but you will not like the technique," Kendrick said.

"What are you keeping from me?" Malus's chin shook, his breathing had become short rapid bursts.

"Hear me and listen carefully to the tenor of my voice. You will find it true and sincere." Kendrick paused to watch Malus's eyes then leaned near Malus's ear. "We followed you for a week. Our observation of your control of the orphans and care for their plight was impressive. Manshire needs *you* to care for the orphans and oversee the schemes we will develop for them. We have discussed land in Saraton to give to the older orphans, an adoption process requiring orphan approval, a traveling education program—all designed to help them feel part of the community and respected, but we need your approval," he whispered.

"Yes, I understand." Malus's shoulders and hands relaxed.

"Wonderful. About that arrow, I am going to push it through your back, cut off the broad head, then remove the shaft through the front."

"I am prepared for the pain," Malus said confidently.

"Do you know why your bodyguard ran from you?" Kendrick asked.

"No. But I think Gora has put a spell on Vee," Malus replied.

The slightest error can cut an artery and kill him, which will surely enrage the orphan army that surrounds this castle.

Hoping Malus was thinking of Vee, Kendrick shoved the arrow through.

"Humphhh." Malus kept his mouth closed muffling a yelp; his face slowly shifted to a light pinkish grey. Kendrick quickly cut off the arrowhead.

"It seems so strange for him to run away from you," Kendrick said as he slowly twisted the shaft while pulling it back. "What kind of spell? Or could it be a potion?"

"Had not thought of a potion."

"The arrow is out."

Dog House

The three outer auditorium doors flew open as twelve rogue combatants charged in firing arrows. One of Malus's guards was disabled—Kendrick could hear the gurgling. He was quite impressed with the other guard who shot two combatants seconds apart.

This was Kendrick's first combat since his return from the frontier. It would be the ultimate test of his left hand treated with Bernard's ointment. Snatching an arrow from the quiver he loaded it above the knot. Holding the bow in his left hand, he drew the string next to his cheek. The shaking had disappeared. He aimed then released the arrow striking the nearest rogue combatant in the throat. Or, so he hoped—it was difficult to tell the combatants from the guards.

An arrow flew over his head and struck a rogue combatant rushing down the center aisle at Kendrick. From the arrow's flight he knew Althea had shot from the choir balcony. *I wish Althea had stayed with Roslyn.*

Was it the heat of the battle, or merely that the rogue combatants were about the same age as young Long Bows that bothered Kendrick? He did not ponder long—he had his children to save.

The remaining rogue combatants plus one guard with Althea and Kendrick filled the space with an abundance of arrows whisking through the cathedral. The enormous cathedral of his youth had shriveled suddenly to the size of a doghouse.

Althea had quickly become a target, but her tactic of ducking, moving to another balcony location, then shooting, though slow, was very effective.

The guard raised his head above the altar and tipped toward the right. Three combatants were maneuvering through the benches toward Malus. Kendrick, crouched between benches, looked to Althea and circled his hand above Malus. She nodded.

"I will be back shortly. Althea is protecting you," Kendrick whispered to Malus.

Creeping slowly up the center aisle toward the statue of Jesus on the cross, Kendrick held the bow in one hand and two arrows in the other. He needed to end this skirmish before Madison and Phyer ignited a full-scale battle.

The main entry door slammed shut. Kendrick spun quickly. An unthinkable crisis required his full attention—Gora held a long knife against Roslyn's throat, the other hand clasped Roslyn's neck. A pale Vee was aiming an arrow at him. Kendrick glanced quickly in the direction of Althea, but she must have been hiding.

"Roslyn, are you okay?" Althea asked, her voice coming from the balcony.

Gora squeezed her neck. "She is fine," he replied. "Now drop your weapons."

Vee's bow was shaking, though his eyes were shining and he appeared to check his balance every few steps. From his short time as a disguised warrior, Kendrick remembered Vee had a deep respect and loyalty to Malus. Gora was truly a skilled deceiver.

"Malus!" Kendrick shouted. He watched Vee's gaze shift from Kendrick to nowhere repeatedly.

"What?" Malus's deep voice echoed in the tall nave.

"I am looking at Vee, he looks ill. Do we spare him?"

"Please," Malus replied.

Grimacing every few seconds, Vee lowered and raised the arrow's tip a couple of inches as he appeared to be battling internal demons.

"Vee. Vee!" Malus's deep smooth voice called out. "I know you can hear me. Gora has duped you and now controls your mind. We have faced many challenges *successfully* these past eight years. I am willing to forgive your recent choices."

"Vee, you know I am the only one that can make you feel good," Gora yelled, his face red with flaring nostrils. "If you kill Kendrick, I will double your portion tonight. You will sleep like a baby."

Vee's eyes focused on something behind him. But what? He heard the arrow as it left Vee's hand and felt the pain of the same arrow as it struck his shoulder. Vee cursed through his teeth.

Fresh blood stained the sleeve of Kendrick's shirt then ran onto his hand before dripping off his fingertips. He reached to remove the arrow but saw Vee had loaded another. He looked into Kendrick eyes and stretched the string a half-inch further.

"Kendrick, drop!" It was Althea's voice but not from the balcony. He twisted as he fell hoping to land on his good shoulder. He caught a glimpse of Althea standing at the bottom of the staircase her feet shoulder width apart, her left profile facing the target and her neck extended as she touched the string to her cheek. Her arrow silently sliced through the air a few inches above his face an instant before Vee yelled in great pain.

Through the leaded clear glass above the altar Kendrick saw the eclipse had progressed to a third of its dark path. The three ribbons were black foreshadowing Madison's death. He kneeled then pulled the bodkin point arrow from his shoulder.

Focusing on Roslyn, Althea drew another arrow from the quiver, but dropped it when a *whooshing* sound passed by her head.

"That was close!" she said. "Kendrick, I do not have a clear shot." *Flaming Dragons.* She glanced quickly at the floor, found the arrow and placed it on the string.

Kendrick jumped two feet to the left and shot the rogue combatant that had targeted Althea. He ducked quickly between two benches just as multiple arrows flew overhead.

When Althea returned her attention to the small, revenge seeking, exiled Gora, he was a much smaller target as he stood behind Roslyn. *No one uses my daughter for a shield! You have placed my son in danger for your selfish pointless revenge. You will never kidnap another child; or lie to thousands of children.*

Althea lowered the bow. *I must thank Kendrick for the archery training.* She repositioned her head. *I can protect my children.* Althea lifted the bow, concentrating on Gora's eyes. *The sergeant said he aimed for the eyes—they never lied.* Gora's eyes revealed fear and desperation. Althea could see the path of the arrow and pulled the string another inch. The arrow struck Gora in the left eye. Althea lowered the bow, watching with horror as the color drained from Gora's angry face.

He was dead. Vee was dead. Another combatant had fallen to the floor.

For Kendrick, the quiet moments after a battle were the most dangerous. He waited behind a bench scanning the room.

A bow and quiver were missing from the combatant he had killed in the center aisle.

Malus was gone.

Suddenly, something sharp pricked Kendrick's skin below the ribcage.

A knife?

"Malus, you learned a lot from Gora. I never expected a trick like this," Kendrick offered.

But Malus was silent. The point broke skin and Kendrick felt a trickle of blood running down his back.

"Okay, you are going to help me escape this cathedral of death, then…" an unfamiliar voice began.

The soft muted sound of an arrow whispered across the still room followed by a thump. Looking over his shoulder he saw the last rogue combatant die behind him, a bloody knife at his feet. *Where had the arrow come from? Who had shot it?*

A quick glance across the aisle and ten rows back gave him the answer. Malus was gripping the back of a bench, holding a bow in his other hand.

"What a shot!" Kendrick shouted, hurrying toward him.

Althea sat next to Malus, wiping Roslyn's tears.

Malus stared at Roslyn. "You are a most brave young lady," he said.

Flaming Dragon

"The skies are getting dark and I can hear the growing rumble of the orphans," Roslyn began.

"We must go before a battle breaks out," Malus asserted. "The orphans will not wait long before deciding to attack on their own. We were driven by the hope for a special place, 'Manshire'. Our desire will not be deterred—we have been anticipating *home* for a long time."

A loud roar echoed through the streets startling everyone in the cathedral.

"Flaming dragons! That is painfully piercing." Althea spread her arms and whispered, "Shhh." After a few seconds she asked, "What is he saying?"

"Ignis—the command for fireballs. He is lighting the fire-pits," Kendrick replied. *Flaming Dragons, they are early!* The scheme was planned so Phyer would arrive at the apex of the eclipse giving the impression Manshire had battle dragons and power to block the sun.

"What makes that awful noise and delivers fireballs on command?" Malus asked. He attempted to stand. Althea caught him before he fell.

"A dragon!" Roslyn said as if he should have known.

"A dragon?"

Kendrick held up his hand, "Malus, is there something we should know about dragons in your world?"

"They are dead. And I suspect my secret guards will remember and organize to kill this dragon preventing it from destroying crops and homes. Still, the younger orphans will be fascinated by it," Malus added.

"My son rides this dragon," Althea said.

"We should hurry," Malus replied.

->>><<<

Twenty orphans were clustered together in a circle, bows drawn, waiting for the dragon to pass again. The cheering orphans reminded Kendrick of the Knight Games audience—loud and rooting for their kin.

The horse drawn wagon, driven by Kendrick, trotted into the outer ward toward the cluster. Althea and Roslyn's windswept hair flowed gracefully with the breeze created by the wagon, but there was fear in every heart.

"Malus, we may need your command," Kendrick said. His heart was pounding; three black ribbons in the darkening sky signified death like the risk Althea had faced at Madison's birth.

A volley of arrows flew from the cluster. Madison ducked and dipped his head.

"Drive faster!" Althea commanded. The two leather straps snapped a moment later against the horse's back.

A bitter smell drifted with the breeze toward the open drawbridge. The stench grew stronger as they approached the fires started by Phyer.

"I cannot sit up," Malus shouted

"Take the reins," Kendrick commanded Althea. "Please."

Kendrick held the reins in front of Althea. An instant after taking control, the thunderous stomping hooves grew louder as she urged the horses to go faster.

He stood and twisted to face the back, always holding the edge of the seat. A rapid look at the sun revealed the apex of the eclipse.

Malus's bloodstained shirt and bandage was sticking to his chest. *I hope he survives this wagon ride.*

The wagon hit a bump, instantly separating the riders from their roost. Althea held the reins but appeared to be flying over the side. "Kendrick. Help!" she cried.

Malus gripped the seat back with one hand, but his flailing arm attempted to find an anchor—in a few seconds Kendrick would be the only passenger.

Kendrick snagged Althea's wrist. He cringed as he pulled her back into the seat, blood was again dripping from his shoulder.

"I am okay. Rescue Malus," Althea said. As she slapped the horses to go faster the wagon lurched from side to side.

Holding onto the seat, Kendrick jumped into the wagon-bed, Malus's free arm slapping his head. He felt the warm sanguine fluid running down his cheek. He did not want to faint. Shaking his head, he caught a glimpse of the arm swinging around for another slap. Kendrick turned into the path of the arm, stopping it against his chest. He placed Malus's hand on the back of the seat.

"Althea, slow the wagon!" Kendrick yelled above the rattling wagon noises, cheering orphans and Phyer's screech. Tugging the reins, it stopped.

Malus stood. The cheering grew louder.

The horse, spooked by the dragon and the burst of cheering, wrenched forward causing Malus to lose his balance. Kendrick strained to keep Malus from falling and his grip on the shirt was failing. Althea quickly tugged the reins and applied the brake.

Madison had turned Phyer around and was approaching the cluster. Kendrick stood in the wagon and pressed his knees against the back of the seat. A large hand grabbed his coat and held him in place. Kendrick circled his hand above his head and Malus yelled, "Cease fire!"

But it was too late as another volley of arrows filled the air around Madison and his dragon. Madison's wail, as the arrow struck his thigh, confused Phyer and he began to dive.

"He has been shot!" Althea screamed.

Madison tugged on the horns repeating, "Terram!"

Phyer screeched and shifted dramatically from right to left. Several times Madison had only one hand on the horns. Still, Madison hung on.

A minute later, Phyer leveled his flight at twenty feet above the ground then lifted his wings in a V. His feet lowered as he neared the ground.

->>><<<-

Kendrick removed the bow over his head and the quiver from his shoulder. He walked to the pit and tossed the pieces into the fire.

"Help me walk to the fire," Malus said. Kendrick wrapped his arm around   Malus's waist and Malus placed his arm on Kendrick's shoulder.

"It is strange," Malus began. "But we never would have crossed the Frontier had Gora's vision not been plausible. He saved us from the monarch who had plans to kill us. Once we started the march there was no turning back—we had burned too many villages. He prepared us for the ultimate battle at Manshire and tactics were analyzed and improved after each battle.

At the fire pit, Malus tossed his weapons into the fire. He nodded toward the cluster, pointing to the fire..

Walking back to the wagon, Malus continued, "He managed the vision masterfully. Parceling the dream of Manshire—land, food, opportunity—and preaching to an eager congregation about equality for orphans. He began his own internal leadership group when our relationship became strained. Vlada's Children's Army was being used to fulfill his revenge regardless of the path the meetings took. And, who knows what he did to Vee. It is peculiar to say, but Gora was the perfect evil prophet."

Kendrick looked to the sky and smiled, in about ten minutes, the eclipse would complete its cycle. "I would like to introduce you to my son. Think you can handle another walk?"

"Yes. I would like to meet him."

With the arrow removed from Madison's leg, Althea was finally able to cry and laugh at the same time. "Being shot in the thigh must be a family curse," she said to Kendrick.

"I need to sit." Malus pointed at the ground next to Madison.

"Madison, this is our new friend Malus. He led the orphans to Manshire." Madison stood to shake   Malus's hand.

"I am happy to meet you. But I think it is time for Malus to disappear. My given name is Luxton. I was an optimistic youth hoping to make my world a better place. Though we need Luxton here Malus has served and completed his duties."

"Nice to meet you, Luxton," Madison said.

"Sit down so I can finish this bandaging," Althea said, just as thousands of orphans emerged from the forest toward the fire-pits. The ruckus was contagious as children large and small threw their weapons in the burning pits and walked to meet Althea, Kendrick, Roslyn and Madison. Luxton's tortured face did not inhibit the orphans' hugs and gratitude.

So many children! Althea's eyes sparkled from her tears as the orphans showed her their drawings of 'Mother'. Many called Roslyn 'sister'.

"Roslyn, do you feel a shift in the mood?" Madison asked.

"Yes. Fear has been replaced with hope and the excitement of a new beginning," Roslyn replied.

Althea looked to Kendrick. He smiled. "Two white ribbons—a new beginning," he said.

Preview of

"Autumn's Rescue"

Coming 2017

The sunlight had just squeezed through the top decking when the ship stopped and shuddered violently. Hannah thought her personal prison would dislodge from its perilous perch above a similar cage and she would land in the aisle once again.

Hopefully, the ship would sink ending this torment.

She had counted the days by watching twenty-two shreds of sunlight move across the floor since being jailed in the ship's hold after two days of confinement on the makeshift dock. It had been pure misery—including the smell of sweaty inmates, the rotting dead bodies, the constant moaning of seasick friends, the beef soup void of chewable bits and the briny water dipped from the ocean. Her stomach ached for solid food. The stench of human waste reminded her of Head Master Ulster's first assigned chore—emptying and cleaning the buckets in the girls' washroom.

Hannah heard the scurrying boots and bare feet, on the top deck mixed with shouts of anger directed at the Sailing Master.

Another jar of the ship sent several barrels rolling across the deck. Loud timber cracking reminded her of crossing the Frontier and getting caught in a storm with the tree branches snapping in high winds. This time her cage fell into the aisle initially leaving her upside down.

Twenty-three fellow captives were removed and escorted out of the hold before her cage was righted.

Hannah cupped her trembling hands around her squinting eyes. A kick to her rib cage had followed the second time; she had scuffed her knees and palms after a guard's shove. Standing, she gaped at her lean shadow. If I go another two days without food, I will die—perhaps ending this nightmare.

When the guards counted twenty captives they were herded to the gangplank. Two guards led the captives then directed them to the hitching posts lining the sundrenched far side of the dock. As the last ropes were tied, another twenty orphans were guided down the plank.

Along the shipside of the dock were fifty open top wooden crates filled with something similar to dirt. Two closed crates were guarded.

"Oh no! I recognize that dirt—it is iron. We are going to be mining slaves," said an older female captive who was slapped seconds after speaking.

www.ingramcontent.com/pod-product-compliance
Lightning Source LLC
Chambersburg PA
CBHW070749180626
46818CB00007B/3048